CONTENTS

Forever Unsheathed

Sexy Stories Collection

VOLUME 42

12 EROTIC SHORT STORIES

SHON GACY

Forever Unsheathed/ Shon Gacy. -- 1st ed.
Xplicit Press, an imprint of TLM Media LLC

ISBN-13: 978-1-62327-573-0
ISBN-10: 1-62327-573-3
eISBN: 978-1-62327-623-2

Printed in the United States of America

1 FOREVER AFTER

It was a beautiful movement, the way it flowed so smoothly and naturally. Their touches intermingling, their breath coming as one, much like the rising of the sun. Adam could see it out of the corner of his eye, like a fireball beginning to light up the horizon. It caused them to pause and wait on baited breath. Knowing what it could do to them if they lingered too long; their motion was in unison.

In the blink of an eye, they were gone, the sun's rays finding nothing but the morning dew to dry up as it reached out is long, golden tendrils. Still, even back in the dusky defines of the mansion, their eyes glued to one another for an instant; Adam wanted something more from her, something far more than what she'd already given. He knew just how to have his wishes taken care of as well. She was naïve to a point, though far more controlling than him. It was something that he simply had to learn to adjust too, but gradually.

He was naked. She loved the fact he was so vulnerable. Still, noticing his discomfort in front of her she decided to go and seek out some clothing for him, telling him she'd be right back. She wasn't sure she'd come back. Sifting through some of the drawers in the spare bedroom, she found some remnants of a past lover's clothing, and holding them up to check the sizes she figured they'd match perfectly with his build. She didn't tally. Coming back downstairs, she couldn't help but laugh as she noticed him standing over by the fire holding a pillow against his protruding cock.

She tossed the clothing his way, and he immediately had to drop the pillow in order to catch them, which she found quite hilarious as well. His manhood was aroused and sticking straight out, much like a visage from a porno flick. It aroused her as well but she didn't let on to him. She was trying to keep a distance, finding it now necessary to lay some ground rules between them.

"Just put on the clothes, unless you'd prefer to stay in the nude. I find it quite...hot really." A blush spread up about her cheeks as he shook his ass, causing his dick to swing from side to side as if in protest. She knew he was intentionally messing with her. He walked to her, stopping almost directly where she sat, almost as if to urge her to reach out to caress him. That'll happen soon enough. She was glad the thoughts come from her subconscious and he didn't have access to them.

He stood there for a long time, examining the clothing until finally he just asked.

"Whose did these belong to? They seem vaguely familiar to me." She cursed out loud, reaching for one of her Marlboro's and lighting it in an angry manner. The smoke pillowed around the two of them as she inhaled hard and then gently blew out twin circles of smoke.

"For God's sake Adam, must you ruin the moment, really? They belonged to Raven but obviously, he isn't going to need them is he? He does stay here quite often, before you even ask me." He sat beside her now, not believing that she had a thing for Raven. She had protested that was in the past. He couldn't help but wonder if she'd really been hiding her true colors all along. Perhaps she wasn't the victim she'd played herself out to be. Their eyes met briefly and he noticed the compassion resting there in hers. Yt gave her a softened look in the light, all the while stirring his emotions even more.

Adam had never wanted someone so much, not as much as he wanted her. He could smell her, so clearly it hurt. He assumed that was how it was once you turned, and the need to fuck was overwhelming. It was another primal instinct he supposed. Her breasts moved under her shirt, with each breath she took. Though they didn't need to breathe, they did it for appearance sake, and to keep some level of humanity about them. He could see her nipples clearly outlined in the sheer silk, and their erection was just as obvious.

When he looked up again, to her eyes, she was staring harshly at him as she finished off the cigarette. "I think we need to get one thing straight here right now Adam. My life is my life, or what is left of it that is. You don't tell me what I can do or who I can see, and neither do I do that to you. Raven would like to think he controls me but he doesn't, and neither shall you."

"So, what are you saying, Teresa, that you would prefer us to not have any relationship at all? Is it that you don't want me to fuck you where you sit right this minute, because I can see it in your eyes? Just tell me, what do you want between us?" His words caught her off guard, as he'd never behaved so boldly before. She found she liked it but it was also rude and uncouth. She was already missing the old Adam. It was her fault though; she had indeed made him what he had become.

"Adam, I told you already, you need to mind your own fucking business. There are things I tell you and things I won't, that is just how it is. Now, when it comes to finding happiness you better be aware that I truly am out for myself. Are there any other questions you want to ask me now? Because I really don't think you want to hear the answers." She was angry, yes, because of his nosiness and lack of respect. It showed. He didn't seem offended though and instead it was right the opposite.

Adam shrugged as he stretched, slipping the silk shirt on but leaving it unbuttoned. He looked more than sexy with the flames of the fire in behind him. She didn't know if he had intentionally tried to sway her thoughts or if it were just something that came easy for him. Either way, it didn't really matter, Teresa told herself.

Adam noticed her eyes dropping to his chest and he knew that she was being lured in, exactly what he'd hoped for. She couldn't stop glancing his way and he would have been lying if he'd even attempted to say her gaze didn't bother him. However, it was she that made the first move, not he. She moved to him in seductive grace, allowing her own top clothing to slip down her shoulders and bare her skin for him, though he'd seen her nude more than once already. She ran her fingers through his dark hair, her nails raking against the side of his neck. Both of their breathing was growing a little raspier with each second.

"You'll find that there is one thing between you and I Adam, and that is our lust we feel. You are like the most vital of honey for me and as much as I try to refrain from tasting you, I can't help myself. Now that you are a changeling, you have to realize that your human laws are gone, distant. This is forever, and while a love might never die in this life, you're not always going to be happy my friend." She paused in her words, loving the way he felt beneath her hand. It caused her to lose her train of thought, even in that odd moment.

Adam had a hold on her before she could even begin to fight back, and when she found herself pinned beneath his broad shouldered frame, she liked it, was dying for it even. Staring into his eyes, eyes that had been friendly in the past, there was that change now. He was not only hungry for fucking but she could see he was truly hungry for blood as well.

When the tip of his tongue entered her mouth it was like hot steel meeting cool water, but it didn't take long for him to heat her up. His hand moved to her breasts, massaging her nipples through the thin layer of material and squeezing when he felt them harden under his touch become hugely engorged for more. He sucked at her there, enjoying her body arch into his as he flicked his tongue back and forth, in the most meticulous of ways. He was intent on having her juices flowing for only him.

"Do you want me to fuck you Teresa, hmm? Do you want me or him?" He didn't let her respond right away as his mouth came crashing down on hers hard and fast. His tongue plunged into her, as if he would have been plunging into something else much warmer and much wetter. As his hand traveled down her body, cupping her pussy in its warmth, her moan was loud and long. She reveled under his touch, enjoying how he could make her almost cum without even entering her. Her own hands had found his manhood, still as hard as before and she ran her fingers up and down his great length, teasing the head of him and enjoying his eyes roll back in pure pleasure from it.

"Take me Adam, and take his scent from me. Replace it with your own if you can." Her words seemed to bring about more anger in him and he rose above her, stretching her legs apart so that his cock could slip in between and lie against her womanly opening. She was wet, dripping wet. As he moved himself against her slit, her heat nearly caused him to cum with the wanting. His breath was in hard pants now, like a dog in heat. He couldn't hold himself back for very much longer at all.

He grabbed a handful of her hair and jerked her face up to his, kissing her as he finally did thrust deeply into her waiting pussy. Both of them were taken away, rising up into the night in the rapture of it. Her tightness, enveloping him and seeming to suck everything from him as he thrust into her harder and harder, so many times he lost count. He could feel her nails raking into the flesh of his chest, the fresh blood pooling. When she bent her head to suck at it, taking her feel she only spurred on his own hunger and thirst.

He bit into the side of her neck, sucking harder and longer. He did relish the taste of her there in his mouth, but was careful to not take too much. Their lovemaking felt it would go on forever in that moment of time, both of them lost in each other so dramatically. Adam could feel that the lust was not just for her but far more. It was almost on the edge of near lunacy that he grabbed her at the hips and attempted to reach the very depths of her as he spurred own, his cock coming to the very edge of her before slowly withdrawing and then driving back in, harder than the last.

"You're a whore, Teresa, nothing but a vampire whore who thrives on driving men to vicious killing for you, but I will show you now, you don't control me." She twisted in his grasp as he drank from her again; bringing her such weakness, she couldn't fight him any longer. The gulps of him feasting on her blood flooded her ears and she knew he would kill her if he didn't stop. Pushing at his chest, while all the while he pounded his cock into her, she finally made him see what he was doing. He stopped right before it would have been too late, leaving her breathless yet still very well aware of him inside of her.

He pulsated there, waiting, holding his breath until he couldn't any longer. "I have to finish, I have too." She didn't try to stop him, but instead allowed him to withdraw from her and take her from behind, working his manhood in and out as he toyed with her breasts in the same movement. Their cries mingled together as they both came at the same moment, her juices flooding with his and ending in a squirting orgasm for her. Adam enjoyed every second of it, and felt more in control than he ever had in his life.

Once she recovered from his draining of her, she wanted nothing more than to lash out at him.

"Do you really think you'll always have things your way Adam? Hmmm? It doesn't work like that. While you might have fucked me tonight, drank from me even, don't think it will ever be so again." He didn't acknowledge her words but rather, he tossed the clothing onto his body she'd given him earlier and walked away. There were no words she could use to harm him, and nothing she could do to stop him. He knew that. He could feel her frustration growing, even though he was now a clear distance from her and up the main hall.

"I'll see you in the morning then Teresa." He'd forgotten that morning meant no roaming around for them. "My bad darling, in the evening then." He laughed as he disappeared from her sight, leaving her to her own musings and ill thoughts but he could have cared less what they were.

He would have his way and he would have what he wanted. Raven might perceive himself to be the leader of their coven but there was so much that Adam had yet to bestow on him either. He had no fear, no worry. In fact, as he lay upon his bed, the blankets a deep soft crimson around him he could only think of one thing. The power. Just as sure as he could feel it coursing through his veins in that very hour, he knew that he could destroy those who would oppose him. He would be seen as a threat but he certainly didn't care, not any longer.

Teresa had taken his real life from him, the one that he'd always known. The people he cared about, how could he ever tell them what he was, and would they even understand? His hands clenched into fists as he thought of all he'd lost but of what he'd gained too. It was one of those situations that you either crumbled within or you grew stronger. There were no half ways.

The shuttering of the windows around him send to go off on a timer and the darkness swallowed him whole inside. His breathing was regular, his emotions in check. The need for rest began to take hold of him, and there in the darkness he waited for it. He knew when he arose he would be brand new, and those who defiled him; they'd have a reckoning they would wish they could run from.

2 THE RED DOOR

They tore into the bags of flour without care, laughing drunkenly as they turned them upside down, allowing the white substance to spill all over the ground. Some of the women ran to try and scoop it back into wooden cups, but were met with forceful resistance, sometimes being shoved back down to the ground, or even stomped upon and kicked. Still, they knew the importance of the food, and they knew the outcome if they ran out of such a necessary food stock.

There were a few that were able to sneak away with some small sacks of it, hiding these sacks among some bramble bushes, hoping that the pillages wouldn't find them. Some of the younger girls were not as afraid of the men as the older women of the village were, and in fact, there were quite a few of them that offered their services freely.

They thought that if they could gain a little coin from the use of their bodies it might give them some hope for survival. However, some of the women were never paid for their sexual offerings, and the men, more often than not, just took these women to the edge of the woods, pinning them against the hardwood of a tree as they rammed their hard cocks into them, pounding away at their soft flesh. When they had their fill, they often just threw a penny, sometimes not even that. It was getting to the point where these traitors to the crown just took what they wanted, when they wanted. It had just been sheer luck for Clarise that she had not been nabbed by one of them.

She could find no comfort with her mother as the woman was as destitute as a barren whore. Her father had been killed during one of the many raids on their village, so Clarise had no one. She fended for herself, sometimes bringing food to her mother, sometimes not having enough to share. It was surprising that given the circumstances she was still very well put together. Her hair hung in long curls down her back, and she managed to keep it clean and combed out on a daily basis. She used the lavender water that she had sparingly, not knowing when she'd see more of it. She'd acquired it from a wandering caravan dealer, who'd stumbled upon their small village. He'd sold it to her very cheap. He'd felt sorry for her, at least that's what she'd guessed. He'd also given her a couple of dresses and sandals, free of charge, and with no questions asked. She'd been grateful, and had told him if there was ever a time he was ever in need he only had to ask. She had no idea how he would ever find her again though, as she planned on leaving the first chance she got. She'd stored up enough loose coins to hop a wagon ride into the royal city, and her intention was to meet with the King to try and get help for her people.

For so long, the Royal Guard had done nothing to help the surrounding villages from marauders, seemingly leaving them out to fend for them. Many said the King was too concerned with invading France to worry about thieves and bandits that were just trying to get by on their own means. Trying to get by. That is all we are trying to do is get by. Yet, the King seemed to not care. She'd heard the rumors about him, how handsome he was supposed to be, taking women to his bed every night. The ones he no longer had any use for, he'd have them done away with. He'd not been able to keep a wife for very long, as his eyes turned to every skirt that passed him by. At least, these were the rumors that floated back to her village about him. She didn't put much faith in what she heard until she could see it for herself. She planned on doing so too, as she'd heard a more recent word that there was a Spanish assembly supposed to be travelling through that area that very day. It was her intent to try and find a way to maybe hop onto one of the wagons without being noticed. Normally the foodstuffs were carried in behind the caravan, so she figured if she waited and watched, she could hopefully earn her own free ride to the Royal town.

She reached for a few of the potatoes sitting on the ground, which had been thrown out of the baskets the women had gathered that day. She also grabbed one flask of liquor that Betty, one of the older women, had hidden among the baskets. She took the only change of petticoats and dresses that she had, and putting her feet into her sandals and turning away from the village, she began her walk down the hill, towards the edge of the clearing, facing the footpath she meant to travel upon. She only looked back once, not having any real feeling for what she was leaving behind. Her life had been nothing but misery for the past few years and she yearned for something more. At the same time, she wanted to try and find some way to help the other villagers, and that was her true goal. She just hoped that she could get to where she needed to go without any trouble. Everyone had said that the road was no place for a woman alone, and the wood, well that was even more brutal. No one wanted to get lost in the wood late at night. There were horrid accounts of people having done that and never being seen or heard from again. Clarise had always assumed that they might have been attacked by wild animals, but then others had said that something far more sinister than that had grabbed hold of those poor souls.

She didn't know for sure, and she didn't think that she wanted to know either. The thoughts just gave her the chills of what could have possibly happened to those who had gone missing from numerous villages. She walked a little ways up the road, checking in behind her periodically for signs or sounds of someone possibly following her. She didn't know how far she had travelled, so wrapped up in her musings she'd been. For an instant, she thought she was imagining the sounds of hoof beats farther back behind her, but as they grew louder, she knew she wasn't mistaken. She hid in some underbrush on the side of the road, not wanting to be seen for two very good reasons. The first, she was afraid that it might be a group of the bandits that so often tortured and terrified the people of her own village, and for the second, she was sure if it was the Spanish assembly approaching, they'd surely run her off the road and out of their way. Lying there in the brush, her heart skipped a beat as she saw the first few soldiers beginning to appear around the bend in the dirt road.

The royal carriage was right in the middle of them all, and then as the first few passed her, she noticed at the end of the procession there indeed were two wagons pulling cargo. Mules were attached to long wooden poles, and they were hauling the wearisome burden. Well little mules, get prepared for a little more weight to drag in behind you. As the final soldiers past, she darted from her hiding place and had to half run, half skip to catch up to the wagon. She managed to get hold of the corner of it and heave herself inside, hoping that no one saw her. There were some burlap sacks atop some of the other items and she covered herself with those, hoping to stay hidden and out of site. It never dawned on her that there might be stragglers to the royal procession.

The movement of the wagon was making her awfully sleepy, and already suffering from lack of food and fresh water, she found herself fighting to stay awake. She had no idea how much farther it was to the city, and the castle itself, but she just had to stay awake. Stay awake. Stay....awake...She felt her eyelids growing heavy, and she thought just closing them for a second or two would be okay, but before she knew it she'd fallen into a slumber.

There was one lone horse approaching in the distance. The rider didn't gallop it fast, but he rather trotted his steed slower than a normal rider would, which almost made him appear suspicious. However, he was part of the group; in fact, he happened to be the Prince in the royal party. He simply didn't like riding with the royal guard, and also, from the back, he could see anything that took place that was out of the ordinary. He was the one who witnessed the girl sneaking into the back of the wagon, and he could see just the top of her head now, covered by the burlap bags in the cart. He had no intention of alerting the royal guard at all. In fact, since they were almost at the castle, his plan was to have her carried to his personal chambers, and then when he arrived there, he would decide what to do with her then. He found her to be extremely enticing, and very bold. It was strange that he would run upon a woman so brazen and fierce from a small little encampment of poor and starving English settlers. He felt sadness for many of them, but then, this wasn't his homeland either. He had no right to just tell the King what he should and shouldn't do, but he was going to advise him.

Prince Vaughn found it awfully distasteful that a King would let his subjects suffer the way this one was. Yet, he had to be very careful how he approached the subject because he knew that their treaty was on the line. He could see the city gates up ahead now, and looking back at the girl, he saw she still had not stirred. He galloped his horse up to one of the guards so that he could inform him of the new, additional cargo. After he gave precise orders of what to do with her, he rode on up ahead, and when the soldiers in the watchtower spotted the approaching royal party, they immediately order the opening of the gate.

As they proceeded into the city square, there weren't that many people about. In fact, it was all oddly still for that time of the day. It was almost as if the city were being punished for some crime that they might have committed. The only groups around were those of soldiers, so approaching a few, he asked where the King was, and it was then he learned of his sickness. The King had been on his deathbed for what appeared to be days now, supposedly coughing up blood and being unable to keep down solid food. Prince Vaughn was told that he would be taken to see the King later in the day, but until then, he was meant to go over the plans that had been drawn out between England and Spain in the weeks before. As Prince Vaughn dismounted, he saw the girl being taken away, thrown over the shoulder of one of his guardsmen. Funny though, he was surprised to see that she did not object to the treatment. Hmm. She quite possibly has some type of agenda.

Clarise didn't struggle that much, basically because she knew it was futile. There was no way she could get away. She had no idea where they were taking her, but she did know that if she did not start devising a plan for a means of escape, or some way to get a word in with the king, she could very well be doomed. The Red door was the only thing that she really saw as the guard entered into the chamber. It was obviously a man's room, as there was the feeling of a man's presence. She asked the guard where she was, and what was happening. He didn't respond, and shutting the Red Door behind him, she heard a key turn in the latch and knew that she was locked in.

After speaking with the King, and seeing the distress that he was in, Prince Vaughn was determined to try and get things in order. It was true that even when the King had been in good health he had not done the things he should have been doing, and due to that, his people were suffering. But, with talking to him and making him aware of how dire the situation was, the King had turned legal authority of dealing with the thievery and bandits into his hands, and he was going to do something to change all of it. As he stepped out into the courtyard, he was appalled at how the tense situation with the people had escalated into what appeared to be an angry mob now. He climbed to the top of the barricade, where some of the soldiers stood with guns at the ready.

"People, people, please... As you know, the King is very ill and I am in command of making certain that all gets back under control the way it is supposed to be. Later tomorrow, there will be an open council for all with ills to come and be heard. I will do my best to make sure you are all treated fairly."

Even after he spoke these calming words there were still those in the crowd that were raising their farmers tools in the air in anger and agitation. Some of them didn't hesitate to speak their mind, even though they knew the penalty for disputing the valor of their King, and not following his laws. Prince Vaughn listened to the many complaints that he could make out floating through the crowd. The majority of them had fallen destitute, and even more were suffering because of the roughnecks that were terrorizing their villages and farms. There were still those that had fallen to disease due to starvation and were now wanting vengeance for their pain and suffering.

Before he climbed back down from the barricade, he told the people once again that he would hear their concerns the following day. If anyone wanted to be heard, or if any needed extra assistance, he would see what could be done to make that happen. They seemed to be quieting down following his second appeal to them, but they weren't dispersing. He noticed that many had made small camps a few miles back from the castle. He could see the campfire's burning in the distance and he could hear some of the more pleasing songs being sung. It was sad to see such unrest in a land that used to be free from such disparity and hate. He didn't blame it all on the King, much of it was due to the continuing war with the French, which Spain had aligned themselves with England to hope and finally squelch that annoying problem.

Prince Vaughn remembered the girl as he made his retreat back to the castle, and entering the foyer, he asked one of the guards if she'd been fed and bathed, of course this particular guard didn't know. So, turning on his heel, he made his way down the long corridor to his chambers. There was total silence around him, and the only sound that could be heard was his boot's hitting the pavement. He stopped outside his room, his hand turning the lock in the latch. He hesitated briefly, before he tossed the door wide. She sat perched in one of the high back seated chairs, looking out the window at the crowd of people that were still swarming around the castle.

As he closed the door, that was when she turned, looking at him intently but without any signs of fear. When he stepped to her, he could see her visibly flinch, so he stopped. "What is your name woman?" Clarise considered not answering him but she knew that would get her nowhere. He was quite handsome, and she herself found him quite pleasing to look upon. His voice came at her in a deep, husky tone. She recognized it as the voice she'd heard speaking into the crowd. He held a powerful presence, and looking at him then, she believed every word that he had spoken to the people.

"My name is Clarise, and before you say anything, I meant no harm stealing into your cargo wagon. My only goal had been to get here to meet with the King. The people in my village are starving, and they are being mauled and killed by traitors to the crown. That was my reason for doing what I did." He stared at her in silence, his eyes taking in her long curls, her bright eyes, and petite frame. She was very beautiful and he felt his body responding to her, even given the situation that she was in.

"Have you been bathed and fed?" She nodded, and he should have known because he could tell now that she was wearing a dressing gown for sleeping, and her skin was almost glowing. He took a place by her, his one foot resting on the frame of the chair.

"So, you meant no harm you say. Why would you have not just stopped my caravan and asked for assistance. Did you not think I would have helped you?" As he talked he toyed with her hair, but she did not pull away. To him it appeared she enjoyed his touch. His fingers travelled down the side of her face, and one fingertip went under her chin, pulling her gaze back up to meet his. A slow blush spread across her face and he realized that he must be embarrassing her.

Clarise found herself wanting him, even though she knew not the first thing about him. She thought to herself though, I've come so far, been through so much. Surely, there is nothing wrong with being loved for only one night. She slid off of her chair, and walked around him in a rather teasing manner. Her hand ran down his chest, and hesitated where she felt his heart beating hard. She smiled up at him, taking one of his hands in hers and placing it on her own heart, which was also beating hard and fast. Prince Vaughn could not believe that she was so willing and so eager to bed him. He didn't know if it was part of her plan to gain something from him, or if it was her sincere desire to just feel a gentle touch, but he didn't mind in the least.

He pulled her to him, and raising her face to his, his lips came down upon hers hard. He teased her mouth with his tongue as one of his hands worked to untie the fastenings of her dressings at her shoulders. As the gown slipped to the floor, he never once took his mouth from her own, but instead he picked her up into his arms and carried her to his bed. He laid her there, admiring her beauty, and enjoying finding a woman that did not seem to be ashamed of openly displaying her body parts to a man's searching gaze. Her breasts were well rounded, and her nipples were hardened from his mouth licking upon them and sucking them. He removed his clothing as well, and as his pants dropped to his ankles, his manhood sprang forward, rock hard and very big to her eyes.

Clarise reached out for him, and gently pulling his cock, she rolled to her stomach, taking the tip of him into her mouth. As she sucked at him there, Prince Vaughn felt the hot pleasure of her mouth was enough to do him in for good. He forced himself to not cum, thrusting forward involuntarily into her moist depths. She took him deeply, all the way to his base, and she sucked him perfectly. With her other hand, she teased his balls, gently trailing her fingers over them, and sometimes cupping and massaging them in her hand. He couldn't stand to have her mouth on his cock any longer, for he knew if he did, he was going to shoot forth his manliness fluids. He pulled out of her mouth, and rolling her to her back, he spread her legs. He licked her thighs, and all the while, his fingers were seeking out that perfect little nub of love, hidden between her womanly folds.

When he did find her, she was swollen with desire, and inserting two of his fingers into her pussy, he found her extremely wet and ready for him. He teased her there for a while, his thumb circling her clit, and his fingers moving in and out of her slowly, but not going inside of her very deep. She arched into him, her eyes closed as she spread her legs further, moaning loudly. Removing his fingers from her, he positioned himself to enter her womanhood, and with one swift, forward thrust he went in deep, feeling her maidenhead give way from it. He'd had no idea she'd never been with a man before so he stopped, waiting for her to move from the pain.

When she did so, she was squeezing her muscles so tightly around him; he could barely take the pleasure. He moved fast inside of her, and when he pulled away, he almost removed his entire cock, except for the tip, so that when he thrust forward again it was a deeper, harder, more purposeful movement. After only a few more strokes of his stiffened shaft within her wetness, he could feel her cumming, her body tightening around him, and her pussy clenching harder and sucking him into her deeper. He wanted to cum at the same time and moving at a far better rhythm, holding her legs high in the air, he fucked her hard enough to make the headboard continuously hit into the wood behind it. His cock found its perfect mark every time, hitting her clit with every stroke forward. She felt him give into it, felt his cum filling her body, and wrapping her legs around his waist she urged him into her wet hotness further, holding him there tightly and ensuring that she took in every drop of his cum. They kissed, his tongue entering her mouth as his manhood still moved inside of her. Their tongues entwined like snakes, each seeking more of the other, and reveling in the pleasures that they were feeling. She had never felt so alive than she did in that moment. He was the first man she had shared anything so valuable with, and she had no doubt about what she'd done. She couldn't be sure that he cared a thing about her, but the way he continued to make love with her, surely he feels something?

When he withdrew from her, he pulled her body close to his, running his fingers up and down her back, and through her long, thick hair. He could not see her face as she had it nestled in the bend of his arm, up against his chest. He didn't speak either, not wanting to ruin the moments that they'd shared. He'd never experienced anything such as what he just had with her, and he was new to these types of feelings. Before he had just taken from women whenever he'd felt like it, but then none of them had ever been untouched by a man either. It was rare to run into a maiden like her, especially with how gorgeously perfect she was. He marveled at that in his own way.

He felt her breathing slowing down, and her heart was not thudding as hard against his side either. She must have fallen asleep. He was exhausted himself, and propping one of his arms in-behind his head he allowed his eyes to close. As sleep claimed him, he could not escape this woman's image, a woman of such divine beauty; it almost seemed too perfect to be real.

3 THE RED DOOR 2

The Chamber

Clarisse awoke earlier than normal, and reaching across the bed linen, feeling for his body, she found he was not there. The bed was no longer warm either, but up above there was a bright red rose on the pillow where his head had lain the night before. She recalled so vividly the time they'd shared and it warmed her blood. The memories of the night before came pouring in. She sighed deeply, remembering his hands upon her skin, and oh so warm they had been. He had brought her to orgasm so many times and she could almost feel the presence of his hard cock still throbbing inside of her. She smiled. He definitely knew how to work what he was endowed with. She loved the fact that he was an experienced lover who knew where a woman's secret treasures lie.

He was a passionate lover, a man that didn't hesitate to ask his lover what she wanted to make her body feel alive. She enjoyed that about him very much. The love that he had kindled inside of her was still very much alive and she almost wished that he would walk in that door at any moment to ravage her yet again. She had forgotten about her main goal, which was to gain aid for her people. She was lost in his face, in this newly awakened emotion that she never wanted to feel. She'd already spoken with him about what her village was going through so she was almost positive he was with the king working out some type of plan. As long as she knew they would be taken care of and protected from outsiders who wanted to pillage what little they had, then all would be well. She could let the rest slide. Clarisse knew it was because of him she was willing to lay down her feelings of animosity to the king, but then again, she had very little choice too. Most definitely, her choices were few, unless of course, she wanted to be be-headed for deviance and treachery of his Lordship. No, I'd rather spend the rest of my days being loved by Prince Vaughn rather than living in a dungeon without light and being tortured mercilessly until my death.

She heard the metal of the door rubbing against the solid hinges before she saw it open. Her heart beat rapidly in her chest, and she found that she was holding her breath as well. As it crept open a little more she blushed, hoping so badly that it was he, coming to give her some more of what he laid upon her body last night. She craved him so desperately. It was almost as if he had put her under some lucid spell, crafted by some well-known sorcerer living within the castles walls. She shivered as a draft of cold air wiggled its way through the crack of the red wood. She pulled the silk sheets around her now, not certain at all of who was approaching for entry in. She'd thought at first it was him, but it was becoming obvious it wasn't as they still hadn't shown themselves to her. Just a second longer and her answer to who was drifting outside her doorway was given. Turning, she watched quietly as two handmaidens walked hesitantly in, and her smile somewhat faded. She wondered why they curtsied to her, and when they proclaimed her name, all her questions were answered.

"Prince Vaughn sent us here to prepare you for the day My Lady," the other chirped in right after her, before Clarisse could say a word otherwise.

"We have brought your clothing for the day as well, as Prince Vaughn chose it himself. He says that he hopes you like his tastes." Clarisse was slightly perturbed at the custom, but then she knew those with money didn't do much for themselves anyway. They were bathed, dressed, hair brushed, humph…sometimes, if they needed help with masturbating, their handmaidens or male servants were used to get them off. They even had sex with them if that is what it took to get hard for their married partner. Clarisse found it vulgar, but then she assumed that she would need to get used to it if she were to be with Prince Vaughn. She realized that she didn't know his first name, and she couldn't rightly go about acknowledging him in that manner. She settled with the common, "My Lord," at least until he could tell her it was okay to call him something else.

She waited for them to prepare the Roman bath, and once they stepped aside, she settled herself into the warming waters. She enjoyed the aroma of the lavender essence coming up from the steam. She took the loofah in her hands and allowed the oiled water to drizzle over her bared breasts. The cool air meeting the warm perked her nipples right up and she reveled in the pleasurable signals it sent to her perfectly parted pussy lips in the water. She ran the sponge down her body, running it between her legs and pressing harder upon her clit to offer up more stimulation. One of the handmaidens happened to notice and stepped forward. She curtsied to her again.

"My Lady. We will pleasure you any way you'd like; we are here to please you." She kept her head bowed for a moment and when she raised it, there was a slight blush across her cheeks. Clarisse decided to take them up on their offer and encouraged both of them to begin pleasuring her body. The one on her left massaged the soap into her breasts and along her arms and back, while the other girl knelt at the side of the bath and drifted her hands under the water and down around Clarisse's thighs. At this point, Clarisse laid her head back on the bundle of linen they provided as a pillow, lost in the wanton emotions that they invoking from her. Her lips parted of their own will, and she spread her thighs for the one who was now fingering her pussy. She hit just the right spots and as she worked her magic, Clarisse closed her eyes, only imagining Prince Vaughn touching her in these places. She'd never before experienced another woman touching her in this manner, and she wasn't ashamed.

She reached orgasm easily, allowing the moans to pour from her lips and arching her pussy into the handmaidens touch. She now ran two fingers up and down her wet slit, wet from the water and her own juicy womanly fluids. She washed her thoroughly, rinsing away all signs of sexual indulgence. When Clarisse stood and held out her arms, they both began immediately rubbing her down with soft towels, ensuring that all moisture was absorbed. The scented oil that they massaged into her skin felt wondrous, and it left a little shimmer atop her breasts, almost a sparkle like. It smelled delicious as well, a mixture of violets and wild daisies. As they brushed her hair out and then began curling it, she felt that she had died and wound up in heaven. She was in such a relaxed state; she could have climbed right back under the silken sheets.

They handed her a mirror and the reflection staring back at her took her by surprise. She no longer looked like the little lone beggar girl that had stolen a ride in the cargo wagon. She looked like the full embodiment of a royal woman, one that definitely held a position. She stood, thanking them for all that they had done. She then watched as they bowed rather demurely, not making eye contact with her, before scurrying out. She supposed they had gone to tell the Lordship that they had finished their duty and she now waited on him to come and receive her. She found she was nervous. After all, hours had gone by now since last she'd saw him and she was beginning to worry that maybe she hadn't pleased him enough the night before. She knew she was worrying for nothing, but yet she couldn't help herself. Anxiety was her middle name, and she was constantly fretting and stewing about something and anything.

She heard him come in as she was seated on the window seat watching the doves fluttering around out on the terrace. She smelled him first, that attractive musky odor that was all him. When she turned, he was beaming it seemed. Happiness was evident all around him, and he was so jovial she couldn't help but smile back at him. When she attempted to stand and curtsy to him, he stopped her.

"There is no need for that My Lady, after all, you are a woman of station, and people shall be curtsying to you." His smile was gentle and warm as he caressed the side of her face. She could hardly believe that this man, this one that she had only known for 48 hours now, was imposing such an emotion on her heart. She felt her hearts stirrings when he was near, and every time he touched her, it sends electric pulses through every nerve in her body. She relished in feeling his skin against hers. She was in love with him; she could feel it. When he knelt over to lightly brush his lips against hers, his hand came into slight contact with the top of her bodice, gently fluttering across the crests of her breasts. She sighed, and held her face against his for just a brief moment.

He bowed to her and held out his hand. "Shall we go then?" She hesitated.

"Go? Go where?" He laughed lightly. He'd almost forgotten that she was not accustomed to what daily activities took place in castles. Well, pretty much they were just lives of leisure, strolling about, attending parties, and eating royal meals. He was sure she would be in awe about it; he only hoped it would help her forget where she'd come from. He'd already spoken with the king, and while he was going to send out the palace guard to drive off thieves and other scoundrels that seemed to be looting villages and families on the roads, he would do no more. Prince Vaughn didn't know how to tell her that the king would only go so far, so he hoped he could avoid it, at least to a point. He could also tell by the look on her face, as they strode out into the hall and she witnessed the beauty that the questions were coming.

She barely touched the top of his hand, but it drew his eyes to her. "So, Prince Vaughn, I've yet to learn your first name. Must I continue to call you this, or is it required?" He patted her hand as they walked.

"My name is Chavin, and no, you needn't keep calling me by such a position. You may call me by my first name when we are alone. However..." They stopped for a moment, and Clarisse waited. As she did so, she watched a little nervously as the many soldiers moved around them, busying themselves with some task she knew nothing about.

"When we are in the presence of others I would have to insist that you hold with the formality, which is simply the way we do things here. Is that okay with you?" She smiled, but it was a rather weak smile.

"So, I'm to be considered nothing more than your concubine when we are among other royal subjects then? Is that how it is to go?" He had a quizzical look on his face as she said this, and he leaned in closer to her, this time almost whispering. It was rather seductive and sent a pleasurable chill down her spine.

"No, that is not how it is between us, and everyone knows it. It is simply how we acknowledge one another, by their position. My Lady, everyone in this castle knows that I plan to take you as my wife." He watched the stunned look come across her face and he enjoyed it. He took even more pleasure as the slow blush began to spread across her cheeks. He walked her into a vacant corridor and pressed her back against the cold cement there, nuzzling her neck.

"My Lady, did you really think that I would ravage you as I did last night and then treat you as a common whore?" He waited for her answer, but she only stared into his eyes in wonder. He saw an innocence there that moved him. There were too few women like her and he never wanted to let her leave his side.

She was going to reply, and as her lips parted, instead of any words spilling forth his mouth was pressed against hers instead, taking her breath with it. He pressed his body hard along her more petite frame, wanting to feel her heaving bosom on his own chest. He enjoyed pleasuring her to no end and could see himself doing so until the end of his days. He himself could hardly believe how she had stolen his heart. Faint footsteps pulled them away, and to her ears, they sounded like they were a woman's steps as they were lighter when they made contact with the castle flooring.

It was his sister, and when she happened upon them, her countenance did not show approval, but when his own obvious disapproval became evident with her she seemed to lighten. She even curtsied to Clarisse, and she to her. Still, Clarisse could feel the coldness around the woman and in that moment, she knew she didn't want to be around her very often. Chavin excused himself from her for a moment, as he stepped away to speak with his sister. It appeared to Clarisse rather urgent, and when he came back around the corner, the look on his face spoke of it. He seemed hurried as he rushed her back to the confines of their rooms. He only told her that she was to stay there until he came back. She had no idea what was happening, but she did hear very loud voices outside the windows. It almost sounded like a mob of people.

When she went to see, she was shocked and dismayed at what her eyes beheld. There was a sea of people carrying all forms of weaponry outside the castle gates. Many were throwing their arms in the air, screaming about how the king had let loose some pestilence upon them. Some appeared sickly to her, or more so malnourished than anything else. It sickened her heart, but yet their actions were wrong at the same time. Her heart beat heavy in her chest as worry over took her. She was afraid that he would get hurt, maybe even killed. That would leave her a stranger in a king's castle, one that she hadn't even met as yet. She sat upon the window seat, holding her chin in her hands as she continued to watch the angry masses.

Her fear was immediate when she saw Chavin step out on the second floor balcony to address the people. She knew that he could be harmed, even with the knights' guard all around him. He was vulnerable to any flying arrow or pickaxe that might be thrown through the crowd. However, she tried to put her mind at ease in the same breath because she saw that it was not him they were angry at. In fact, at his appearance they even seemed to settle down as they listened to his words, some asking him questions on what the king was going to do, or what he was going to do on his own. She listened intently for a while before finally becoming so sleepy she moved to the bed. She removed her clothing to lie on the silk sheets, as the heat was awfully oppressive bundled up the way she was. She knew it wasn't customary to sleep nude, but then she wasn't familiar with all of the royal people's customs to being with. She also told herself she'd lie anyway she wanted to. After all, she was in her own private bedchambers. As her eyes drifted closed, she thought of him again. Before sleep over came to her, the thought lingered in her mind of what he would say or do if he happened back into the room with the current state of dress she was in? It left a silent smile lingering on her lips as sleep did finally claim her.

4 THE RED DOOR 3
The Resolution

There was an uprising coming, Chavin could feel it in his bones. As much as he honored his position alongside the King, he was not willing to put neither his life nor Clarisse's life on the line. Though his words at the speaking had seemed to squelch an uprising that night, who was to say what would happen in the next day or two? His nerves were on edge and he could feel the many guardsmen's nerves rattled as well. Though no one spoke of it, it was certainly obvious in many of the faces he passed.

Chavin had no intention of letting such hate and animosity spill over into his newfound life. He'd looked too long and searched for so many years for what he'd just come across. Sometimes he still believed it to be a dream, at least until he would feel the sting of reality creep back in on him. He had valued the King at one point and time, but things had changed. He didn't want to be a part of that change either.

The Kind had already retired for the evening and Chavin was told he didn't want to be disturbed. *Doesn't want to be disturbed hmmmm?* He decided to have a message drawn up with his seal at the end. No one was to open it but the King himself. Chavin planned on leaving that very night, taking Clarisse with him as well. The King had given him the Oriental Gardens Estate down in the Eastern part of the realm and far from the chaos of the city. It had been done in good will, a sign of peace between France and England. Chavin had already authorized the support of French troops for the King, but he doubted how well that would hold up in the brunt of the fighting. In the end, France was sure to leave England standing on its own. That was just the way of it.

It was better for him to separate himself from all the politics, and even the religious fancies that were happening. The unrest was certainly unnatural. He had never seen anything like it himself...the riots and slayings all around the countryside. What was sad was the fact that they bothered the King none. As long as he was safe he seemingly paid little heed to the suffering of his fellow countrymen being treated cruelly and barbarically. That is where he planned on going, at least until everything died down and the people came to their senses. He could only hope that would happen.

He stopped by his sister's chambers only to find that she had already left with her guardsmen. There was only the message lying across her bed begging him to seek peace somewhere else. The siege on the castle was apparent, it was going to happen. He attempted to keep a visage of calm about himself as he passed the King's guards on his way through the courtyard. He'd already told his men to prepare their horses. Though dusk was settling he was leaving before night fall.

He found her asleep upon his arrival, her face so peaceful, and restful in her slumber. She appeared just a child lying the way she was. Chavin didn't know how long he stood admiring her like that, but when she suddenly stirred and her eyes fluttered open to find him there a smile spread across her face. She reached for him and of course he wasn't going to turn away from her.

He was shocked to find her unclothed beneath the silken sheets, and apparently she'd been waiting for him for quite some time. Still, they didn't have time for love making just then. Just as he was to tell her what was happening she pulled his face to hers, her own lips soft as velvet and her breath like a whisper. It simply drained his will.

"Chavin, I've been thinking about you so long....all day you've left me alone." He kissed her back, enjoying the sweetness of her mouth, the smell of her flowing into his senses.

"Clarisse, oh sweetness. I wish we had time but we have to leave here, now." She stopped, her eyes staring back at him so innocently. "Leave, but why? What is supposed to be happening?" She sat up, forgetting that she was undressed. The blankets fell away exposing her taut and perky breasts and causing him to take a deep, ragged breath. She was absolutely stunning and he so wanted to fill her right then, but they were certainly wasting time.

He lay across the bed with her, his one hand running up and down her back as he thought. He could have taken her then, in that moment too. He so wanted too. He could feel her femininity through the thin fabric as she turned and pressed herself into him.

He sucked in a sharp breath, leaning a way to contain himself. Chavin attempted to turn his mind to the matters of immediate concern. He could feel her eyes on him though, seeming to seek out his deeper emotions. He ignored her for that moment, at least the best he could.

"You surely heard the commotion earlier today. The people are more than upset and aren't going to stand for the King's blind ignorance any longer. I've received word that the castle is going to be besieged, and more than likely the King will be killed or taken prisoner."

"So, we are going to be okay? You can get us away?"

He whispered to her, calming her and building up her faith in him. "It'll be fine, and yes. I will get you out of here safely."

He helped her dress, loving seeing her creamy skin moving against the palm of his hand as she allowed him to help her. He simply pulled her shifts and camisole over her head and wrapped her in one of the silk blankets to keep off the night chill as they hurried down the castle halls. There were some guards still lingering but most had disappeared. Chavin assumed they had fled.

His own men were outside the gates waiting on him, the carriage already set up for Clarisse. He hurried her to it and placed her inside, turning to his men to speak with them before they left. He could see the King's chambers from where they stood. There were no torches lit, no candles visibly burning. He could only assume that he was still asleep. They had their own plans, and that didn't include traveling on the main roads either. He figured that would lower their risk of running into plunderer's and other forms of bandits at such a time of unrest.

Chavin quickly joined her in the carriage, pulling the tail of the blanket in and shutting the door soundly. They were on the move before he had fully settled in the seat beside of her. Watching the scenery go by in the quiet of the night as they were, it was almost as good as a fairy tale could get. She moved a little against him, still halfway asleep. Chavin was sure the motion of the carriage was like a lullaby to her at that moment.

He nuzzled her neck gently, all the while, pulling her closer to him. He could feel her breath against his neck, arousing him even more. When her eyes finally did flutter open, his face was in her full line of vision. She sat up slowly, adjusting the blanket and her own clothing beneath it. He truly was enchanted by her, her beauty, and simply...everything. She was like no other woman he'd ever known. *And how many has that been?*

"Where are we at Chavin?" He smiled at her, glancing out the carriage's open window for a second before turning back to answer her. She was like that of a child, so wide eyed and full of wonderment, despite what was happening so far behind them. He could only imagine in that moment what could possibly be taking form.

"Well Clarisse, we'll be at the Oriental Gardens before the morning. Halfway there now."

"Really, that is amazing!" She'd heard so many stories about the beauty of the Oriental Gardens, and the wide sweeping lands surrounding them. The castle was supposed to be more beautiful than one from Cinderella's story. She kissed him gently on the lips, lingering there for a moment longer than she needed too.

"So, Chavin. When we arrive, are we going to be alone? Will we finally have just ourselves to focus on and nothing else?" He smiled once again at her, loving her naïve innocence as always. She had a childlike wonderment to her when she took a peek outside as well. The cold air felt good against her face, and it reminded her that the winter months were certainly upon them. She longed to be in a secure place and certainly hoped they would be. The terrors were enough to last her a life time and she was ready for a new beginning.

She moved closer to Chavin, seeking some of his comfort and warmth which he willingly gave her. Her eyes were heavy, and the steady rocking was sending her back to sleep. Perhaps it was best. When she felt his arms close in around her, and felt his deep releasing breath she felt more than safe.

Chavin was tired himself, as they'd been traveling half the night. It would be morning soon, and lying his head back against the cushioned seat of the carriage, his thoughts wandered away, far from where their bodies lay resting against one another. He remembered their first kiss, and as he began to doze, his thoughts remained focused on that thought, allowing for the sweetest dream ever. Why not anyway? Weren't they finally on their way far from the reach of the rebels and the chaos that was bound to grow worse?

Her skin was as white as snow kissed grass, glistening under the morning rays. With her hair splayed out around her she was the pure image of seduction, his little vixen. She smiled up at him as he stood over her, his clothes falling to his feet, scattering around her already nude body. There was an early morning chill, but neither of them seemed to notice it. As his body was lain across hers, his lips caressing her face and then falling to her lips, they were lost in the love for one another that was overwhelming, binding them together.

Neither of them had known one another very long, but that didn't matter and it certainly didn't still their growing passion. She kissed him, hot and heavy, and of course he didn't stop to consider his own response. It simply happened. He wasn't urgent to hurry their lovemaking, after all, why rush it? Even when she moved herself against him, grasping his arms to raise her body to move against his, he didn't attempt to push her back and move inside of her. Though the pressure of desire was building in his loins, up to a crescendo, he controlled his body. Her sweet smell; the taste of her as he took his first, sweet nibble of her pussy with his lips. She was more divine, like the sweetest of nectar. When she bucked against him, moving her small little treasure mound harder into his tongue, he flicked at the bud harder as he pushed one finger deep inside of her wetness.

It was the rickety motion of the carriage knocking his head to and fro that stirred him from his drowsy state. He hadn't meant to fall asleep, but then, exhaustion waits for no one. He noticed that she was curled up against him, her head pressed firmly in his lap. Unintentional as it was, her breath was blowing directly against his clothed cock, he could feel it as her chest rose and fell. His stirrings were obvious too as he was as hard as any dick could become.

Grunting slightly, he moved her, shifting his own position to try and ease the uncomfortablness of his condition. *Soon enough vixen...soon.* He didn't know how much farther they had to go but surely it wasn't very much longer. He couldn't take 3 more hours riding in the confines of the carriage. The sun had slowly began to rise off in the East too so Chavin knew it had to be the wee hours of the morning, around 6 am he supposed.

Just as he had been contemplating their time, he felt the carriage beginning to slow and knew then that they were arriving outside the gates of the Chateau estate. As it came to a purposeful halt, and he heard the horseman mumbling some obscenity, he stepped out, putting a hand to his brow to block the light now growing brighter in the distance.

Turning back to the carriage he extended his hand to Clarisse he looked every bit as exhausted as he felt even though she'd slept for quite a while. She was still beautiful, and as the morning light fell upon her it just seemed to illuminate her features. She was like a vision from a dream floating to him.

Clarisse was flabbergasted by the beauty of his home. It was extraordinary, and just as he'd said, it was far away from all the craziness back hours in behind them. She couldn't help but wonder if it would eventually find its way to where they were though. Still, looking up at him and the friendliness that was visible in his eyes, she felt it was best to enjoy their solitude for the short period of time that they might have it.

Chavin watched her every move, the flitter of her eyelashes as she somewhat closed them to shield from the early morning light. The way she stood with one hand slightly at her hip when he spoke softly to her. Even the way she held her head as she walked. While she might not have been from noble birth she acted just as proper as any of the other high class ladies. In fact, he was happier with her than any of those who had tried to bed with him. She was that one, he knew it.

They were both quiet when they entered into the master bed chamber and the sitting room which went along with it. She noticed there was a terrace, and wanting to see the view she half ran to it, throwing the thin doors aside and stepping out. Chavin joined her there, wrapping his arms around her from behind. She smelled good, and felt good too. Now that he had her all to himself, away from the stirrings of revolt he knew exactly what he wanted from her.

His kiss said it all and she melted into him, standing there in that bright morning light. It felt that they had all the time in the world to just luxuriate in the passion that they had found in one another. However, Chavin knew it wouldn't last and unrest would come whether they wanted it to or not. Still, it wasn't coming that day, and as he laid her down atop the plush silk bedding, grinding his hardened passion into her, all thoughts of anything else left his mind.

How long could it stay that way? Would it stay that way?

5 UNSHEATHED 1

New Love

Monet took one last look at herself in the dulled glass outside the bar before she strode on in. She was so self-conscious of her body, yet every man that she encountered became entranced by her looks. She thought her eyes were her best attribute, as she wasn't fond of her bosom being overly large. She felt disproportioned in every way. She smiled at Brock as she entered, noticing how his eyes traveled up and down the length of her form.

She really wasn't dressed any differently than she always was, other than the fact that she was wearing a soft pink shirt which had a lower cleavage than others she owned. Her hair was worn a little differently too, piled high atop her head with the curls falling down each side of her face. Though she knew she might appear more appealing than normal, she still didn't like the fact that men didn't seem to understand how to keep their senses about them when they crossed paths with a somewhat pretty female. "I doubt Brock thinks I'm the most gorgeous woman he has ever seen," she thought.

Her mind was always talking back to her, but she never let on that her thoughts dominated her conscious every moment of the day. She sometimes felt lost and alone, which she realized was the sole reason she'd given herself to Don that one night. Don had been one that was very dominating, but that was of course understandable as he lived a hard life. He was a gunslinger that she'd just ran into in the bar that one time. There had been an immediate attraction between them, and she had found that he had brought a smile to her face, something that was very seldom there. He had admitted to being a gunslinger, and he'd killed many people, but that one fact had slipped

Monet's mind as she heard the sad tone of his voice, the sultry sound of it having filled her ears with other thoughts. Of course, now he was long gone, but his image stayed in her mind. She could still recall that small bit of time they'd shared so long ago. Monet remembered his lips, because they had been the best part of him, although the grey of his eyes has been rather piercing. She remembered too that although he hadn't talked an awful lot, he had spoken volumes with his eyes. But those sweet lips he'd had, oh the pleasures they had brought forth in her. He had been her first lover, in fact her only one, and her body was still burning with what he had taught her.

He had never rushed the evening, but rather, he had taken his time with her, showering each small section of her skin with his mouth. When he'd reached her breasts, he'd groped them in each hand, and had sucked at her nipples with his tongue in ways that had sent her womanhood begging for more. He had her reach climax more than once with him, as he had known exactly what to do and where to touch her to make her come alive. His manhood had been so big, and he'd worked it so well inside of me. Her inner thoughts brought a blush to her cheeks, and she felt her body become enlivened with the heat of them. While he had ridden her all night, from behind, on top, the side, every which way she could think of, he hadn't stayed with her. He'd apologized for taking her virginity, but he told her he just wasn't a man who could stay in one place for very long, and in that case, he had only been traveling through for the night.

Since that time, she hadn't really paid men much attention, feeling that they all wanted only one thing and that was not what she wanted for herself. While her body always became excited, and yearned for those feelings of arousal and pleasure when she saw good-looking men strolling into the bar, she never approached them. She knew that they watched her, and some even tried to get her to sit with them when they were drinking, but she always declined, giving them some excuse about this or that. Monet knew that not many people could relate or understand her life circumstances. Many of the townsfolk felt sorry for her and how quickly she'd had to grow up, but none really took the time to intervene and make her life easier either. Her life was hard, and it took a strong will on her part to get through the day-to-day worrying and hassles of it. Still, she was happy in her home, and she was thankful that she had sustenance and decent clothing to wear, unlike some of the other's that often ventured into Lily Valley.

Monet had been raised by her Uncle and he had always been nothing more than a town drunk. The sheriff had locked him up on more than one occasion, and on those times when he hadn't, he'd always been bringing whores back to the house. She recalled one evening in particular where she'd sat in her room, hearing him whoop and holler, telling the whore to suck his cock harder. Because the woman had been so loud, Monet had heard her oohhhs and ahhhhs late into the night, begging him to fuck her harder, and to take her in her ass. She'd found it quite disturbing, but now that he was gone, she also found that she missed those wild and crazy times too. She was a woman on her own, and for women on the frontier, that was a very dangerous scenario if you had no man that could come to your aid. However, her Uncle had not showered her with any form of reasonable knowledge, especially on how a woman should behave. He'd never helped her understand what a woman's position was really supposed to be, so due to that she was somewhat of a tomboy type of female. Some of the wagon train hands that came in always commented on that, because very rarely did she wear dresses and skirts.

Monet was far more comfortable in boots, tight rawhide pants, and plain white shirts. She found her shirts hard to keep clean, but she loved the cotton feel of them, and she enjoyed the fresh scent of the material. She used a lavender essence soap to wash her clothing, and after she'd hang it out to dry, it just appeared to her that the essence of the lavender enveloped itself within the crispness of the fabric. It made her feel feminine, even if she didn't dress the part. She didn't wear any form of binding around her breasts either, so her movements always brought attention to her large bosom area. Monet didn't consider herself fat, but didn't feel skinny either. The other females told her she had one of those builds that were to die for, a curvaceous form that sent the men's heads spinning. She didn't know how much of that was true, but she did appreciate their comments. It made her feel good to be told she was attractive, even if she didn't believe it at all.

There were many things about her that did make her stand out more than other females would. She could ride a horse just as well as the next man could, and she loved going riding, it was the one place where she could feel really free. She also knew how to lasso a horse, something very few women could do.

She carried a gun, which she felt was a necessity, because again, being a woman out there alone, she had to have some way to protect herself. She could shoot well too, and this intimidated some men. As she sipped on her beer, again, something very few females did, she could see that a crowd had formed over at the corral, and hurrying up, throwing down the coin necessary to pay for her beverage, she stepped out into the bright mid-afternoon sunlight, walking at a steady clip to see what the entire hooray was about. As a shot rang out on up ahead, she hurried her steps, but at the same time she didn't really know what for, it wasn't like she'd be able to stop a fight at all. Or can I?

There were no women in sight when she got there, just a huge barrage of men, and cutting through them all she stepped to the center of the scene, finding two men encircled in the crowd yelling curse words at one another. One of them had pulled his gun, it was still in his hand and the smoke was billowing up out of its end. She recognized Roy, he was always a loud mouth troublemaker, but the other one, she'd not ever saw him in town before. There was a long scar that started at his jaw, and trailed down to his chin. There was a definite mysterious air about him, but there was more than that. For the first time since Don, Monet found she had interests in him. He was very arousing to look upon. He wore his gun holster lower than the other guys in town did, which signaled to her that he was probably a gunslinger, just as Don had been, They always carried their weapons a little lower, so that they could draw them faster if they needed too. His eyes were what really drew her to him, as they were as dark as the storm clouds building in the sky, even though evening was beginning to settle in upon them.

Monet pushed the rest of the way through the crowd, and before she realized it, she'd pushed so hard she had entered right into the center of everything. The stranger's eyes fell upon her, and she immediately began to get flustered, but turning her back to him, she turned her attention to Roy.

"What the hell are you doing Roy?" When she looked at him, the distaste upon her face was obvious. He was not a very good-looking man, and his teeth were awfully yellowed from the constant chewing of tobacco. Of course, it didn't help him any that he never cleaned them right, nor did he take baths regularly.

"What do you care Monet, this ain't your concern, now you need to step your snide ass aside, fore's I shoot you too." At that, the stranger came forward, and catching Roy unaware, he landed a punch square in his nose. The sheriff seemed to appear out of nowhere too, hollering for everyone to scatter. As the men began to disperse, and the sheriff hauled Roy off by the scruff of his neck, that left her and the stranger standing alone in the midst of the dirt street. She noticed he kept eyeing her suspiciously.

"I just didn't want anyone getting hurt, that's all." She held her hand at an angle, to block the sun from her eyes. Tony couldn't stop himself from continuing to stare at her in awe, she was mighty attractive, and her eyes were like spun gold in the sunlight. As the cloud cover continued to roll in, it took away some of the light, and it appeared at that point the color changed to a deeper brown as she met his.

"What are you looking at?" she asked.

He chuckled; her fire was something to really be reckoned with, and she wasn't like other women, he could tell that right off.

"I'm simply looking at you Ma'am. I can't help but not to with that fire of yours, and those brazen good looks."

Monet looked away, embarrassed but intrigued at the same time. He stirred a fire within her that hadn't been that hot since she'd had Don inside her. Looking back at him, she decided to just go for it, she had nothing to lose.

"You want to go back to the bar and have a beer? I don't know your name, ummm..." She waited for a moment. "I'm Monet." He held his hand out to her, and when she placed hers within it, it was an immediate pulse of desire that raced through her. She drew away pretty fast, and she couldn't tell if he had the same reaction to her or not, but there was indeed something.

"I'm Tony, and yes, I'd love to go and have a beer, but, are you sure you can handle some?" She threw him a look that could have spit daggers, nodding assuredly.

"I might just drink you under the table. Come on, let's go." With the dimming sun at their backs, they both made their way to the bar together, talking animatedly along the away. Monet liked him. He was easy to talk to, and he seemed like the first decent man that had come through in quite some time.

⊗

She ordered a shot of whiskey instead of beer, and while waiting for it, she propped one hand under her chin, totally enthralled with just watching him. He seemed rather hardened, and didn't appear to her to be the type of man that knew that much gentleness, but then what man really did. She'd never met one that was all soft and gushy.

"So Tony, tell me - how long are you thinking of staying in town?" He leaned back in his chair, propping his booted feet atop the table, and twirling a cigarillo around in his mouth, he half smiled at her. This one is just full of questions. He pondered how he should answer, because he really had no idea himself how long he planned on staying. He guessed it depended upon what he was going to be getting in return; and the way things seemed to be going, it already looked favorable.

"What can your town offer a lone drifter Monet?" He caught her off guard with that question, and it must have shown on her face as she called for Patrick to bring her another whiskey. Tony excused himself for a moment, and going to the bar, he asked where they had lodgings for the night.

Patrick really didn't like offering a room to someone he didn't even know, and then, knowing he was spending time with Monet left him soured as well, but when the gent pulled out a roll of money, just seeing that took any questions away. He gave Tony a room key and passed him Monet's shot of whiskey too.

57

"You can take this to the lady when you go back." Tony tipped his hat at the man, and turned, eyeing Monet from behind. Her ass was nice, well rounded in her chair. He loved the shape of her body; curvy in all the right places, and when he came back around to the front of her, handing her the shot of whisky, he already had the question he was going to ask her formed in his mind. He'd been on the road for a long time, and he was tired. He hadn't bedded a woman in months, and there was something about her that he was in awe of. He didn't care too much about all the tender chitchat, or the soft kisses and touches. When he had a need, he only thought about fulfilling it, and looking at her, he could see himself spending quite a bit of time in Lily Valley. He didn't have to be to his cattle herding for another month, so...

"Monet?" His voice was rough, raw feeling evident in it. She was unsure now of what he wanted, and she had the bad feeling that this was all turning into the same thing that had happened just 6 months prior. She was at the point though where she didn't really care, and when he simply angled his eyes in the direction of upstairs, she knew what his intention was. She rose from her chair, following in behind him, her body already on fire with curiosity. His ass looked good when he walked, and his shoulders appeared much broader as well. When they were concealed from the other customer's view, he didn't hesitate to pin her in a position to where she couldn't move. His breath was hot against her skin, but he smelled absolutely delicious. She held eye contact with him, and then broke away as her eyes took in the embedded scar that was so deep upon his face. She raised one hand, tracing the indention of it there, but only for a second, as he yanked it away, holding it against the wall in behind her with his own. She could feel the urgency in him, as well as slight aggravation. She'd known before hand, having watched how he acted when she talked with him that he wasn't the lovey-dovey type. She knew it was too late to back down now, and she didn't think she wanted to either.

"You want it, don't you?" Monet was pinned to the hall, his body smothering her with its warmth, and creating stirrings deep down within her that she hadn't felt in a long time. He pressed harder into her, grinding his now bulging cock into her own womanly desire. He took one of his hands, and aiming her face up at his, staring intently upon her for just a moment, he moved in. She could not speak, and when she tried to turn her face away, she could not, he kept her in that position so his mouth came down hard on hers, demanding she open to him. She parted her lips, and his tongue darted in, instantly seeking satiation from hers. He groaned with need, and pushed his body against her entire frame, his cock aching now as the taste of her filled him. He breathed in her essence, the smell of lavender invigorating him, and driving him to have to have her. One of his hands cupped her breast, massaging it under his palm, as two of his fingers teased her nipple to hardness beneath her blouse. She couldn't stop the moan escaping her, couldn't keep herself from responding back to him, as she arched away from the wall to feel the full, growing length of his manliness. She caressed him there, through his trousers, loving how she felt him move. Oh, he is so fucking big. She already wanted him, wanted to know what he would feel like within her, thrusting his manhood hard and fast into her velvet warmth. She felt the wetness growing, her desire pulsating, demanding to be fulfilled.

"Let's go, now." She didn't hesitate, and as he made his retreat down the hall, she was his for the taking. He held her hand within his hurrying her alongside of him. Her body seemed to sense the pleasure that she was going to be experiencing as her heart began pumping harder in her chest. Looking at her hand caught up in his, she loved the site of seeing her much tinier one nestled there. His skin was a dark golden brown compared to her fairer complexion. It looked nice, and looking at the back of him, she couldn't stop her mind from running away with itself. She knew she'd just met him, but she'd just met the drifter she'd bedded months prior too. She told herself this time would be different, that she would have him forever. But in the back of her mind, she already doubted those beliefs.

He wasted no time when they entered into the small confines of the room. Shutting and latching the door in behind them, he turned back to her, and instead of taking the time to unbutton her shirt one button at a time, he ripped it open, revealing her breasts to his hungry eyes. He immediately took them in his hands, sucking each nipple simultaneously, moving from one to the other, swirling his tongue around the little nubs and bringing them to hard erections. He unpinned her hair, letting it fall freely around her, making her that much more enticing to him. Her pants were nothing to remove as he just unholstered her gun belt, letting it fall to the floor. Her pants fell with ease. He stood back, admiring every quality about her, and when she stepped to him in a bolder way, taking his face in both her hands and placing her mouth upon his, he felt his heart soften just a little bit, but his cock only hardened. She reached for his belt buckle, his gun already lay to the side, and when she had removed his own pants, his cock burst free, falling into her waiting hands. She loved the feel of how heavy he was with his girth. He was the biggest that she'd seen, and with that only having been Don, she had little to compare it too. She ran her hands up and down his length, teasing the head of him and squeezing it a little harder than the rest. Her tongue played with his own, twirling about it like a hungry woman. He pulled her away, just so he could run his own hands down her body, stopping at her most sensitive of places. He fingered her between her silken folds of womanly flesh, finding her little tiny nubbin and rubbed it hard. Two fingers slid into her, and he immediately found the most sensitive spot, stroking it up and down with his now wet fingers.

He groaned in need, and picking her up in his arms, he carried her to the bed, releasing her atop of it and letting her drop to the mattress. He climbed on, and kneeling slightly in front of her, his cock hit the tip of her mouth. When she made contact with him she could see what he wanted, and not looking away, not even for an instant, she let him slide into her moist depths, sucking at his head, and licking at him. He leaned back, enjoying the sensations of her mouth stroking up and down him. She moved faster as he began to thrust himself into her moist center, but just as she felt he was going to cum, she pulled him out, bringing the head of him instead to her pussy, and rubbing him up and down her opening. She allowed the tip of him to ease in just a little, and it nearly did her in. She was on fire with the want.

"Ohhhh, Tony! I want your cock in me!" He pushed her hand out of the way, and parting her legs wide, he plunged into her, moving hard. His cock felt as if it were hitting the edge of her very womb, as he went as deep as he possibly could, their flesh smacking into one another. A think sheen of perspiration formed on his body as he worked it harder, pumping into her over and over.

Monet was in utter heaven, and as she wrapped her ankles around his waist, she raised her pelvis higher, allowing his cock to hit her sweetest spot.

"Ohhhh, just once more, once more!" She knew as soon as he plunged forward again she was going to explode, and that she did. She screamed in pleasure as her cum squirted out, spilling even onto his thighs, which didn't seem to bother him. She could feel his own body tensing, and when he hit into her harder, holding himself deep within her, she felt his hot fluid filling her. She sucked at him hard, urging him to move even further into her warmth, and he didn't hesitate. When he rolled over, he brought her with him to where she was now sitting astride his cock, and as she began to move her body on top of him, she knew this wasn't going to end any time soon. Leaning down upon him, she sucked his tongue as she worked her pussy on him, bringing him to hardness once again.

6 UNSHEATHED 2

Survival

Monet loved how he felt in her body, as she rode him on top now. This was the ultimate experience for her as it gave her complete control over his every movement. She leaned down occasionally kissing him deeply as she gyrated on him, always moving. Sometimes she clenched her muscles tighter around him inside of her, feeling his manhood move and quiver within her pussy. At times, he would move in a way that felt like he was gliding directly over her sweet spot inside, sending her body shivering in response. She took his hands and placed them upon her breasts, loving him squeezing and massaging her. He was able to take one into his mouth as she leaned over him, and his tongue wrapping around its hardness felt just too good to her.

She moved her body faster now, up and down on his wet dick, wet from her cum.

Placing her hand in behind her, she sought out his balls, teasing him by rubbing them and rolling them through her fingers. She was careful not to put too much pressure because she knew how easy pleasure could turn to pain. His moans were coming faster now, and he grasped her by the hips, now raising her up and down on him through his own movements. She cried out as he went deeper each time, almost touching the very edge of her womb. On the last downward thrust she clenched around him, again shooting forth her cum all over his member. She could feel him cumming too, feel his hot seed filling her body. She rotated her hips on him, grinding her pussy into his pelvis, and allowing her clit to rub against his public bone. He was so big, and his cock could hit every corner of her pussy, pleasuring her in ways even Don hadn't even been close to coming to.

When he pulled out of her, she was a little saddened by it, but he pulled her body to lie against his side, wrapping his arm around her waist, and running his fingers up and down her back. She snuggled closer to him, the smell of their sex filling the air. She didn't find it repulsive; in fact, she found it to be quite the turn on. She turned her face up to him, noticing his eyes were closed. She gyrated her ass up against his still partially hard cock, trying to coax him back to attention. It didn't take but a second, and his eyes were wide open, his hand coming across her body and massaging her hard nipples, still erect from their passionate lovemaking. He raised one of her legs slightly, easing the tip of his cock to her moist center, and without question, he thrust himself inside of her. He was able to easily tease and play with her breasts as he moved, and in the position he had her, he was able to move deeply, feeling every inch of her pussy. When she pushed back on him harder, gyrating in circles on his hard member, he couldn't stop from cumming. She was so damn tight, he couldn't control himself, and he was really too exhausted to even try to stop it. Wave after wave of pleasure took him over, and the more she squeezed her pussy muscles around him, the more he lost control. When he had spent his last drop inside of her, then and only then did she loosen her grip, allowing him to slide out. She was so wet from their lovemaking, and wanting to clean off, she rolled over, saying his name again.

"Tony?" The only response she got was a slight, "mmmm," and so she didn't say anything more. She simply watched him lying there so peacefully and trusting. Their bodies fit together like the perfect puzzle pieces, nothing was out of whack. It was the same thing with their joining; they seemed to be made for one another. She rolled to her back, reveling in her experience, and running her hands along each side of her body. She enjoyed the feeling down in her pussy, the humming of passion beginning to subside just a little while, but her nipples remained hard and ready for more sucking action. He had a way with his mouth to where when he sucked at her, it send pleasurable feelings all throughout her body. She rose to a sitting position, throwing her legs over to the side, and allowing her feet to dangle over the edge of the bed.

When she turned to look back at him she noticed he was staring at her. Something akin to curiosity seemed illuminated in his eyes. She smiled at him, and he smiled back. There was warmth settling around them, and it appeared that their feelings for one another were welcomed by the other. Monet stood as she began picking her clothes up from the floor and started putting them on. Just her shirt at first, as she went to the wash basin, dipping the wash cloth in the water and gently washing between her legs, and slightly inside of herself. She could feel his eyes on her the whole time, and she couldn't help but wonder if what she was doing was exciting him, watching her cleanse their sex from her body. She finished dressing, and had just gotten to the door when his voice stopped her.

"Where are you going?" He asked, startling her for a moment and she kind of jumped a little, making him laugh. She acted as if she lacked experience in the company of men, but he wasn't going to dare ask her how many she'd known. He felt that was none of his business. He watched her eyes travel down his body and stop at his bulging cock under the sheet. She giggled, putting a hand to her mouth.

"Hard again Tony? I thought I'd go down and get us both something to eat and drink." He rose up on one elbow, enjoying her wanting to please him. He didn't want her getting too close to him though, he was already aware of how bad that was an idea health wise. He didn't want her to get hurt and he knew other gunslingers could show up looking for him there. He reached out for her hand, running his fingers in the palm of it, and causing the hairs on her arm to stand on end.

"Be careful, okay?" She looked at him puzzled. "What should I be careful about?" she couldn't figure him out. Monet simply smiled at him, walking out of the room, and shutting the door quietly in behind her. As she approached the stairs going back down to the bar she could hear numerous male voices down below. Stepping into the shadows and peering downstairs she could make out three rough looking riders. They all had guns; all wore their cowboy hats in that rugged way that seemed to somehow fit the demeanor of a gunslinger. The one in the middle had a deep, husky voice, and he almost sounded threatening when he spoke with Patrick. She could make out one word, and it was "Tony." So, they were looking for him.

Monet looked back up the hall, wondering if she should go and let him know that there were these strange men downstairs asking about him. She began to wonder about his past and about what he might have gotten himself into before he came to town. She had met others like him before, coming into town, acting shady, and obviously having something to hide. She had known from the get go that there was something off on him anyway, but she still couldn't put her finger on it. Tony didn't look like the type that ran with riff raff, and he didn't look like the type that enjoyed taking someone else's life either, but the characters down stairs surely did. She moved slightly to the right to try and gain more of a view and when she did one of them just happened to glance in her direction. He saw her move and didn't hesitate in announcing it to his buddies.

They all turned, looking in her direction, and when she knew for a fact that she had been discovered, she moved out of the shadows. The one in the middle eyed her more intently than the other two did, and Patrick looked scared to death standing in behind the bar. In fact, to her he appeared to have a thankful look come over his face, seeing their attention diverted elsewhere.

"You, where did you come from?" It was the middle one, and he spoke to her in that deep husky voice. At any other time, she might have found him sexy. He had blue eyes and curly blonde hair. Another plus for him was the fact that he had all his teeth and they were perfectly white, unlike his buddies who appeared to have brown nubs sitting inside their mouths. Monet started down the stairs, failing to have replied to him as yet. She didn't break her eye contact though, and it seemed to make him uncomfortable as he shifted his weight from one foot to the other.

When she got to the bottom he motioned her over, and she made a mental note to be very cautious, because she noticed his hand move down to his gun holster. She of course moved her hand to feel for her own, and then it dawned on her that she had left it upstairs. At a time when I needed it the most, damn it! What is he going to do? She noticed that he had followed the movement of her hand, and when he glanced back to her face she could tell that he knew she normally carried a gun. He had a strange expression, like every man did when they found out that she had her own weapon, and especially when they learned she could shoot just as well as the next guy. Monet noticed that Desmond, the bar keep, looked scared out of his mind, and Monet tried not to let her own fear show. When the middle one motioned for her to come over to where he stood, she did so without question.

"So, where did you come from, hmmm?" She felt his cock pressed firmly against her ass and didn't like it at all, but what was she going to do. One of the other men had a bottle of whiskey in his hand and he turned it up, taking a long swig of it. He already appeared drunk as he did his stupid little giggle, climbing upon one of the tables and dancing around like some dumb ass. When he tossed the bottle against the far wall, sending it shattering into pieces Monet knew that Tony was going to hear it and immediately figure that something was definitely amiss. The taller guy had come up beside of her, flicking her hair with his hand and laughing in her face. His teeth were nasty looking, with some of them missing and what was left hanging there rotting and distorted.

"So, sweet stuff, maybe we should have a little fun with you. After all, there isn't anyone around to stop us, now is there?" He swung her around to face him, his face directly in alignment with hers. He wasn't ugly at all, but he was abusive, something that she didn't take too kindly too. The fact that she didn't like being pawed upon like he was didn't help either. "Why don't you tell me who is upstairs, and save yourself a little bit of the pain and agony that is surely coming your way if you don't tell me right now."

"I'm not telling you anything you fucker. Now take your hands off of me!" Before she saw it coming his hand backslapped her, knocking her down at his feet. He grabbed her up by the arm, jerking her back against him. A slight trickle of blood was falling from her mouth. She could taste it building up inside too.

"Look bitch, I'm only going to ask you once more. Who the hell were you upstairs with, because I know you were up there fucking around, I can smell him on you." Monet looked at him strangely, wondering how in the hell he could smell anything at all. She knew he was messing with her, the smirk across his face spoke volumes, and his eyes squeezing up into slits spoke of his ignorance. She felt his body becoming enlarged, that manly part of himself seemed to have no will of its own as it hardened against her ass. He even gyrated himself into her, and when he continued she laughed in his face. It seemed to make him angry but instead of hitting her, he moved one of his hands to her breasts, squeezing them hard, and feeling her nipples through her clothing. She tried to twist away again, but he just held her all the tighter.

"Hey boss, why don't you let all of us have a go at her. She ain't worth nothin' anyway. I'd like to give her some of my hard meat." The main one just laughed at their comments.

"Ain't no one having her until I get my fill, then you can do what you want. It ain't no matter to me; she's just a whore anyway." When he called her that word, the one word she hated more than any other, she spit in his face, watching it slide down his cheek. He hit her again, this time across the cheekbone, leaving a small, open gash from the ring he was wearing.

"Bitch, you need to learn your fucking place." He pinched her nipple hard in between his fingers, causing her to wince in pain, but she did not bend to his will. Just as he was getting ready to undo his pants to fuck her, movement from upstairs stopped him. There was a loud crash, like a door flying open, and then heavy booted footsteps. She was going to call out to Tony to not come down, but before she could this guy had clamped his hand tightly across her mouth. He motioned to one of his partners to take a crouching position in behind one of the over turned tables.

Monet heard him coming down the stairs, and she kicked and bucked frantically against the man holding her, but he only tightened his grip on her. When Tony appeared at the base of the stairs and saw the man holding her, the blood on her face, she could see the anger flashing in his eyes. He had his guns and she knew that it meant trouble.

"Why don't you let the girl go, Tim? She has

nothing to do with you and me." In that moment, the one that had been hiding moved up in behind Tony, pressing the barrel of the gun into his back. Tony spun around, bending the guys arm back until the bone audibly crunched, visibly jutting out from his forearm. He fell to the floor, rolling and moaning in agony. When Tony turned back to face the guy named Tim, he had his hand on his gun, ready to shoot. Monet was sure that if it wasn't for her in the line of fire, he would have already pulled his pistol.

The man jerked her head back hard, yanking her hair and bringing her down to her knees. Tony snarled, anger filling him, yet having no means to help her. He knew that if he pulled his gun she would get shot. Tim motioned for him to turn around and he did. He also finally released his grip on Monet throwing her to the side like a doll.

"Let's go Tony. You know your payback is here, and I ain't playing no games with you, you slimy bastard." As he approached Tony, he was unprepared for how fast he moved. Tony lunged, his gun drawn, hammer cocked. There seemed to be a double gunshot, and as Monet watched in horror, not only did the other guy crumble to the floor, but so did the man she knew she had fallen in love with. She screamed his name, running over to him. There was a pool of blood forming underneath him, and she could see he had been shot in the side. He looked weak, and as tears pooled in her eyes, she cried for someone to get help.

The barkeep ran out, screaming for someone to get the doctor. It felt like an eternity to her, there holding him in her arms. She could see he was in pain, and getting weak. "Tony...please...please"! As a group of men came running in, she noticed one of them was Doc Adams.

She ran over to him, tugging at his sleeve. "You have to help him, you have to! Please!" They carried Tony away, back upstairs to the room were, just an hour before they had shared in each other's bodies. The tears were flowing freely from her eyes now as she thought of what it would be like if she lost him now, the one man who had changed everything for her, who had made her feel like a woman again. She'd never known you could come to care for someone so deeply, so quickly until she'd met him. For the first time in her life, she prayed, prayed like she truly believed. She knew it was all in God's hands, and in her mind, she was beginning to really wonder if he truly existed. One of the girls came over to help her to her feet, pulling a chair out for her. She could only sit in shock and wait. Wait to know if he was going to be alright. Wait to know if he would be the same if he did live. Never in her life had she been more afraid than then. Sitting there, a quiet settled around the place. It was so still you could hear other's breath, but then she realized it was herself breathing so heavy. A calm settled itself around her heart, and when it did, she felt at peace. Somehow, someway, she knew everything was going to be alright, it had to be.

7 UNSHEATHED 3

Forever

Monet sat at his bedside, sometimes getting up to wipe the sweat from his brow, and other times to gently wipe the perspiration from his arms and legs. She couldn't sleep, and when she did doze, his moans woke her. The doctor had told her she needed to go and get some rest, but he'd been saying that same thing for days now. She'd told them all she wasn't going to leave his side until he came back to his senses. There were some days where he would partially open his eyes and try to speak, but she didn't know how much of her he was actually seeing.

She didn't even know if he really knew she was there. The doctor had said his fever was so high he could easily be hallucinating which was making it appear he was opening his eyes but really, it was just a reflex action from the fever.

Monet didn't believe him; she didn't believe

any of them. It appeared to her that no one thought he was going to pull through his wound except for her. She had already witnessed a miracle with him just surviving. Of course, he was going to have a battle ahead. She leaned over his body, placing a kiss upon his lips and allowing hers to linger there for just a moment. As she pulled away, she noticed his eyes were open once more, and this time he seemed to be watching her.

"Tony?" She fell to her knees by his bedside, taking one of his hands within her own. She ran her fingers up and down his arm, trying to coax him into more awareness. "Tony, I'm here baby...I'm here."

His mouth opened and she could see he was trying to say something. She rose, and leaning over, her ear at his mouth she heard him audibly say, "Thirsty." She didn't stop to think to go get the doctor; she was so wrapped up with caring for him and tending to his needs.

She brought the water glass to his lips, holding his head up just a little for him. He took a sip, but some streamed out the corners of his mouth, as he was too weak to swallow it all. "It's okay Tony. Take your time. I'll be right back." She hated having to leave him but she knew she needed someone to go run and get the doc so he could check his vitals and temperature. It appeared to her though that Tony was going to make it, and her heart was doing a dance of joy in her chest. As she opened the door, looking back at him, he still was watching her. She passed a weak smile at him and half ran down the hall, leaving the door open.

Her voice echoed off the walls as she half-ran, half-jogged down the stairs. "Someone get Doc Ham, its Tony. He is awake. He really is awake."

Paul, one of the local ranchers, and some other fellas were the only ones in the bar at that time. He didn't hesitate to get up and rush out, promising her he'd hurry back with the Doc. With that confirmation, she raced back up the stairs, taking two at a time, just to get back to the man that she now knew she'd fallen in love with. She didn't know when it had happened or how, but that didn't matter. She loved him and without him, she just didn't want to live. She was shocked upon finding him sitting on the edge of the bed when she re-entered the room. She ran over to him, encouraging him to lie back down, which of course he did. Still, in his weakened state he reached out for her.

She kissed him on his mouth, his forehead, his neck, and his hands, whispering to him how worried she'd been. "You're going to be okay baby, you're going to get through this. I'll be here to make sure of it. I'm not going anywhere." Just as she had completed her sentence and stood back up, she turned around to find Doc Ham trotting into the room with his black bag in hand. He seemed to have a look of wonder on his face, and as she moved to give him room, she made it a point to let him know how wrong he'd been about Tony's recovery. He simply waved her off, not wanting to admit his wrong diagnosis of his patient. She watched as he listened to Tony's heart and lungs, having him rise up so he could listen to his lower lobes.

"Well, everything is sounding good." He put his stethoscope back in his bag, but before closing it up, he took out a small bottle of pills. "Take one of these, every 4 to 5 hours for pain, Tony, and you should be on the road to recovery. There was a small piece of the bullet that we couldn't get out, but I think it is okay, it isn't going to be able to shift and go anywhere as far as I can tell." Tony nodded at him, and Monet could tell that he was starting to feel some soreness even then. He shook the doc's hand, and Monet moved aside to let him pass.

"It appears to me that you have a wonderful nurse here taking care of you as well. You're lucky!" Tony laughed a little, grabbing his side when he did. Monet waited for them to leave before she went back over to his side. She immediately dipped the cloth in the basin of water at his bedside and began wiping his face with it. She would have kept doing so if he had not stopped her by placing his hand on her wrist, smiling all the while. She noticed he winced a little, too. When she reached for his pills, he stopped her.

"No, I don't want that now baby, but you could do something else for me."

She raised one eyebrow, wondering what in the world he was hinting at. When he threw the covers back, trying to slide over a little bit, she stopped him.

"Now, you know you can't be moving all around like that, hun. Have you lost half your mind while being unconscious?" She leaned over, inspecting his bandages, which were all clear, showing no signs of any bleeding from his wound. She ran her fingers across his chest, circling around his nipples, which seemed to get hard from her movements. She winked at him, but didn't stop.

"Monet, you're not helping me here." She followed his eyes down to his manhood and immediately noticed he had developed a hard on. Laughing lightly, she encircled him with her hand, softly running her fingertips around his tip and teasing him a little.

"Tony, surely you're not ready for that?" He smiled at her, throwing the covers back even more, tempting her to climb on top of him. There was no way she was going to do that though, not after all he had just come through. Instead, she scooted closer to him, close enough to where she could taste him. She started at just his head, sucking at him gently. She made sure that he could see everything she was doing, too.

She moved her mouth slowly at first, taking him halfway into her mouth now as she allowed her tongue to glide across the underside of his cock. She felt his sharp intake of breath, and felt him move in her just a little. When she started moving up and down his length, sucking harder and then letting up, his body arched just a little. She knew he wanted more so she moved faster on him, sometimes removing her mouth all together to stroke him with her hand. Every once in a while she moved to his balls, taking one at a time and sucking them as if they were hard candies filled with some secret treat that she was dying for. Indeed, she was dying for him. She wished she could have him inside of her, but that was next to impossible given his condition. She moved up his body, placing her mouth over his and kissing him deeply as one of her hands never left his cock, stroking it faster, harder all the while. She whispered in his ear.

"You like that baby...hmmm...do you want more? I'll give it to you if that is what you want." She slowly moved back down him, stopping in spots. The first visit was sucking at each of his nipples, licking their hard, erect tips before traveling back down to his abdomen. She let her tongue flick into his belly button once before moving to his thighs, kissing him and nibbling on his skin there. When she took his cock back into her warm mouth, she knew he wasn't going to be able to last. She moved hard and fast on him, in a way that was reminiscent of their lovemaking. The sucking noises filled the room, along with their moans of pleasure and want. When she felt him cumming, she made sure to go all the way down on him, directly to his shaft, sucking and releasing until he finally exploded into her and she swallowed all of his manliness, not worrying about the saltiness, but only about giving him pleasure.

When she was done, she wiped the corners of her mouth and sat back, not complaining at all about her own needs. She covered him back up after cleaning him off with the washcloth. She was so tired herself, but there was no way she wanted to leave him. Her stomach growled loudly, and Tony even heard it. Again, he tried to laugh, but it simply caused him too much pain and he quieted.

"Why don't you go down and get you something to eat, I'll be alright." She had a much better idea than that.

"No, how about I go get us something to eat and bring it back up here. We can have a meal together. I like that better." She was holding his hand in hers, loving the way that it felt, and simply loving being able to do so again.

"Whatever you want to do is fine. Can I have beer?" Monet looked at him like he was out of his mind.

"No, not with the meds Doc Ham gave you Tony, you know better than to even ask. I'll be right back." As she walked down the hall, she couldn't take the smile off of her face. She knew that everything was going to be okay now. She didn't stop to think of anyone else that might be after him, she didn't want to. She was all too aware that the life of a gunslinger had its perils, and she had just encountered one of those. Still, they both were standing, despite the odds.

She passed Pete, one of the stable hands on her way over to the Silver Spoon, the only decent restaurant in the entire town. She enjoyed chitchatting with him as he was always smiling and seemed so content with his life, unlike so many other people in town. When one of the brothel girls came out to put an arm around him, Monet simply shrugged, walking off. She heard the girl holler out something about staying away from her man, which Monet thought was pretty darn stupid considering everyone already knew that she herself had a man and she sure didn't want Pete, as nice as he was.

The Silver Spoon was definitely busier than normal, but then again, it was lunchtime. Many of the cattle rustlers had come in to town to grab themselves a bite to eat before running back out again. She ordered up some taters and beans with the fire-stoked cornbread. Standing there waiting for the order to be finished, she watched some of the couples strolling by through the window. She thought of herself and Tony walking along the streets like that together one day soon, and it brought a smile to her lips. Jenny noticed, and as she handed Monet the food she wished her and her man well.

"Thanks Jenny!" Monet had never felt so lighthearted in all of her life. It seemed to her that all of the pieces had finally fallen into place and she didn't want it any other way. She hurried back to the rooming house above the bar, her heart beating hard in her chest as she took the stairs as fast as she could. She'd been gone a little longer than she'd anticipated and was worried that Tony might have tried to do more than what he should. Entering into the room, she found him sitting at the edge of the bed again, combing his hair.

"Tony, what are you doing?" She rushed over to him, forcing him to lie back down.

"Damn Monet, you have to let me breathe a little." She smacked at him playfully as she handed his food to him.

"I'll be more than happy to let you breathe when you are more able to move around on your own. Now eat up." He had a ravenous appetite, which wasn't surprising considering he had been out of it for a good number of days. He finished his food long before she did, and she became so self-conscious with him watching her, she just sat hers to the side. Washing her hands, she had a thought come to mind, and as she began removing her clothing, she could see him watching her from the corner of her eye.

"Don't get any bright ideas Tony; I have my own game plan here." He simply laid back and smiled at her. When she climbed into the bed with him, she was so careful not to nudge his injured side to hard. When she did climb on top of him, he looked taken by surprise. She laughed wholeheartedly, feeling his cock rising against her pussy. She was already wet with excitement and couldn't wait to have him inside of her.

She half moaned as she spoke, holding his hard, rigid member in her hand and running it in between her legs. "You wanted this, and you know damn well I want it, so I'll just have to be extra gentle with you." When she had the tip of him inside of her, she sighed deeply, loving the way he felt there. As she allowed her body to slide down his length, sucking him up inside of her pussy, she couldn't stop her body from arching back and almost screaming out in pleasure. When she moved, it was slow but steady. He kept his hands on her hips, encouraging her to continue riding him. She stayed more secured to his member, more so than moving up and down.

She rotated her pussy on him, using a circular movement, while he played with her tits, sometimes sucking at her hard nipples, turning her on all the more. When she leaned farther back, he grasped her breasts in his hands harder, flicking his thumb and forefinger across each nipple. He could feel her meeting him in orgasm, her body tensing and squeezing around his cock, seemingly pulling him in deeper to her warm, wet depths. She sucked every drop of him, her body shuddering on his now semi-hard manhood still buried deep inside of her. When she rolled off of him, they stayed connected. When her eyes finally closed from sheer exhaustion, she fell asleep with a smile on her face, feeling this is where she always wanted to be, right next to him for the rest of her life.

8 OCEAN'S EDGE

The air was balmy against her skin, and her thin silk shirt clung to her chest, outlining her firm, well rounded breasts. Sarah wore no bra, she'd never liked the feel of being confined in one, so she let her joys be free, her nipples reveling in the warm air as they hardened under her shirt. The flight had felt like an eternity, and she was ready to get to her hotel and just relax.

The first thing she planned on doing was stripping down to her birthday suit, and stepping out onto her balcony facing the ocean. She had reserved her favorite chalet on the island, and, in times past, had often walked nude along that strip of beach at night, sometimes even stepping into the ocean's edge, and enjoyed the feel of the tropical wetness against her skin. *"Maybe I'll do that again,"* she thought to herself, smiling at the idea. *"It will feel so good."*

Sarah was definitely an uninhibited woman. She was a free spirit, believing that the body was there to enjoy, and seeing clothes as a barrier to that pleasure. There had been so many times she had pleasured herself, just simply sitting in a restaurant waiting on her entree to arrive. No one had ever been the wiser, but whenever a male waiter had walked by, even one with average looks, she had automatically began thinking of what their cock would feel like in her throbbing pussy. The men she had dated had all been intimidated by her abrasive attitude and her need for sexual fulfillment all the time. She smiled to herself as she gathered her luggage, recalling Henry, the last affair that she'd had before coming on this very trip.

Henry had been extremely good looking, but he had been flawed. He had never been able to fully sexually satisfy her, and he really hadn't been interested in oral sex, something that she just couldn't ignore. If she was going to be with a man, he had to want to eat her pussy. There was just no getting around it. The feel of a man's tongue on her lips, oh... Sarah shivered in pleasure, remembering others who had not had a problem giving it to her. She felt there was absolutely nothing more perfect than feeling a man's tongue going to town on your clit, while he fucked you with his fingers at the same time. Oh, the orgasms she'd had! Now, she found herself alone, without a man, and seriously in need of one.

Sarah had grown tired of never having a permanent relationship. She longed for someone to wake up next to in the mornings.

She wanted to wrap herself around them, fuck them if she wanted, and do whatever she wanted with them every single day, but alas, that wasn't how her life was turning out. She was a beautiful woman. Her hair was full, curls boundless, and her eyes were greener than the trees themselves. She had one of those bodies that men simply couldn't resist, but it just seemed when they learned of how excitable and wanton she was in the bedroom and in public, they just couldn't deal with it. It was surprising to her, since men were often saying that there were too many cold fish out there. Once they seemed to get a hold of a real hot-blooded woman that loved sex, they couldn't handle it. Although, that didn't really surprise her. After all, men were known to break their promises.

Her heart was heavy though, and as the taxi cab driver loaded her luggage into the trunk, she couldn't help but feel her heart sink a little, as she got into the cab alone. Here she was, in an island paradise, but with no one to share it with. Now, how sad was that? She vowed one thing, as the cab began to roll into motion, and she saw the cabbies eyes strolling down her face, and centering themselves on her breasts; she was going to have as wild of a time on this trip as she wanted, and there was no one who could tell her otherwise.

As the cab rolled to a stop in front of the

hotel, he came around to her side of the car, opened the door for her, and stepped away so she could exit the vehicle comfortably. She smiled at him as she stretched, aiming her face to the sun, and reveled in the warmth. This island was truly a tropical paradise, full of lovers, and full of mystery. She could see the top of the tiki bar from where she was standing, and turning to the cabbie, she asked him if he could take her luggage into the resort for her, which he kindly obliged. She slipped him an extra $40.00 for a tip, and waving bye to him, she meandered on down to the tiki bar. Everyone was familiar with her at the resort, so she didn't worry her luggage wouldn't get to where it was supposed to go. All of the workers had already been aware of what time her arrival was, so she knew she could trust them to take care of it for her.

Normally when she stayed at the Chardon House of Sanctuary, they already had silk linens on the beds, and the balcony doors opened to step out on the terrace, as they all knew she loved the ocean breeze coming into the chalet. She took an end seat at the bar, and laying her purse down, she spun around, looking out into the bright blue sky; the sound of the cresting and crashing waves taking away the stress from reality. She absolutely adored being right there at the Ocean's edge, there was nothing as beautiful in the whole wide world to her, than this very coastline of beach.

Sarah noticed the dark haired man before she even sat down at the bar. He was chatting with some other women, and their conversation appeared fairly animated, with the girls sometimes laughing loudly. She let out an exasperated sigh, and propping her head on one of her hands, she saw Tommy approaching her. He was rather cute himself, but she'd been vacationing there so often, she had become quite used to him, and saw him only as a friend. She just couldn't bring herself to see him in any other light, no matter how tight his ass was in his pants. He also had a nice size bulge in the front part of his britches, and she didn't know if she was the cause of it, or the girls in their bikinis were.

He gave her a welcoming smile as he approached. "How are ya', Sarah? You haven't been out here in a while. I hope the world is treating you well?" Sarah simply sank lower in her seat, now propping her chin on both hands, mumbling something about stress and no life under her breath. She ordered the banana colada, asking Tommy to put in an extra shot of vodka. She felt it would calm her nerves just a bit. Through the corner of her eye, she noticed the girls were finally walking off down the beach, and the dark haired stranger seemed to be eyeing her with interest. She tossed him a half smile, turning her back to him, and thinking how she didn't need another inconvenience. Yes, she was looking for a hot hunk to ease her troubles, maybe to have some fun with, but she didn't want another loser on vacation.

Sarah swung around as she felt a hand touch her back and, elbow jutting out, accidentally hit him in his nether regions. He doubled over in pain, a loud "ummph" escaping his partially opened mouth, the toothpick he'd been chewing on falling to the sand. Sarah immediately rose from her chair, going to him, and stroking his back.

"I am so, so sorry! I didn't know you were right there. You startled me. Are you okay?" He coughed, holding his balls, his face red from pain. "Here. Let me help you." She took him by the arm, allowing him to lean on her, helping him to the seat beside hers. She sat down again, asking Tommy to bring him a shot of tequila to take the edge off.

"I can't tell you how very sorry I am. I didn't mean to do that. Gosh... I hope you're going to be ok?" She waited for his reply, and noticed that he seemed to be regaining his composure. When he looked at her, it was with a sincere interest, even though the pain was still there behind his eyes. She could tell he was masking it. When Tommy brought the shot, he downed it in one gulp. He leaned back, massaging his crotch, and apparently not caring if she saw him or not.

Of course, Sarah understood why he was doing so, but still... He was making her hot, as he seemed to have no inhibitions about him at all. He finally smiled at her, and extending his hand, he introduced himself. "Well, I'd like to say that it is a pleasure, but of course..." he paused, slightly motioning to his balls, making Sarah laugh. "I'm Douglas. And, you are...?"

"Oh, I'm Sarah. It is very nice to meet you, even though we probably wouldn't even be having this conversation if I hadn't hit you in your privates there." Sarah covered her mouth before she burst out laughing, but he showed no signs of indignation at all. Instead, he seemed to be taking a quick once over of her own goods. She blushed self-consciously, but she knew too, she had a damn nice body. So, sitting up straighter in the chair, she pushed her breasts out more, the nipples obviously erect behind the sheer fabric. The fact that she wore no bra left little to the imagination. But Douglas still found just enough hidden skin to keep his interest piqued.

Clearing his throat, he leveled his gaze and looked at her face. Smiling widely, seeming to have recovered from the pain to his groin, he waved his hand about, not pointing at any one thing, "So, Sarah, are you like me and find yourself just intoxicated with the ambiance around here or what?"

"It is quite breath-taking, yes. I must say, I've never seen you around here before, and I visit the island quite often. Have you ever vacationed here before?"

'Should I tell her that my ex-wife and I often visited until she dumped my sorry ass?' he asked himself, smiling hesitantly. Opting not to her about it at all, he nodded slightly. "I haven't been here in a while, but I felt it was time to take a trip back to a place where I could reminisce. It's been quite some time since I've been here." He paused for a moment, clearing his throat again, partially from being nervous, and just out of sheer habit for the other. "How long have you been coming here?" he asked, hoping to change the topic.

Before she could reply, Tommy jumped in for her, swinging his legs over the bar, and plopping his ass down on the counter-top. He chuckled lightly as he scratched his unshaven chin. "Sarah has been coming here for years. She visits about every 3 or 4 months, says it's the best island experience out of any place she's ever been." Sarah shot Tommy a rather shoddy look, irritated that he would offer her information so freely. Douglas looked amazed.

"So, you must know the people pretty well, not only here at the resort, but on the Island in general?"

"Yes, yes I do. I'd say so after having been from one corner of this island to the other. The people are definitely friendly and lighthearted, and just well, totally loveable! The people here at the resort are the best." She picked her drink up, and taking a long sip, she motioned to Tommy to get her a fresh one. There was a breeze coming in from the ocean, and it was very exhilarating to her.

Tilting her head up to the sun, she enjoyed feeling the warming rays on her already tanned face. Douglas found it quite sexy how she arched her neck. To him she seemed like the type of woman who didn't mind what other people thought of her at all. It was quite refreshing. He couldn't help but imagine how she would maneuver her body if she were fucking him. Her breasts were pushed out so far; he could have reached out and cupped them in his hands, if he had wanted to. Her nipples were extremely hard under her shirt; he could see the dusky tips of them poking forward. He couldn't help but wonder if she was aroused by him, because he was certainly aroused by her. His cock stirred with thoughts of her lips encircled around it, sliding up and down his thickened flesh. He turned away from her for a moment, as he had to quiet his mind. He certainly didn't need to get a full hard on standing there in the open, but if he didn't stop, his entire crotch was going to be jutting forward to say "how do you do" to her.

As Tommy passed her a fresh drink, she took a good swallow of it, savoring it on her tongue, and enjoying the feel of it as it slid down her throat. She eyed Douglas from the corner of her eye, noticing that he was watching her every movement, which made her just a tad uncomfortable. Still, she was happy to have a man showing her adoring attention again. It had been quite some time since she'd felt wanted in this way. She stood, stretching her back as she did.

"Well guys, they should have my chalet ready by now, so I'm going to head up and take a shower, enjoy the view and just kick back. She grabbed her purse off the bar, and as she turned to walk away, Douglas's hand came to rest at her elbow; pausing her in motion for a split second. It was like slow motion as she turned back to him, a quizzical look upon her face.

"Perhaps I'll walk you up to your chalet Sarah. I really don't have anything planned."

It took her by surprise, as after all, they'd just met. Still, her body was yearning to feel a man's touch on it, and he was a hottie. She gave him her most teasing, cat like smile, almost purring when she replied. "I'd enjoy your company, if you don't mind."

Douglas didn't mind at all, and as they walked off together, Tommy had to hold back the jealousy that was barely hidden. He'd been harboring feelings for Sarah for quite some time, but she'd never showed him any real favor. *"Let a stranger come along, and she's all over him. Bitch,"* he thought, but didn't really mean what he was thinking. He had grown so tired of waiting for her to see that he was interested in her. It just seemed to him that he wasn't good enough for her kind. After all, she came from the big city, obviously had money, though he'd never asked her about all of that, and she was one of those classy broads. Tommy was just a laid-back bartender and surfer in his free time.

The women all thought he was hot enough, but he'd noticed that the majority of the women that came to the retreat were all looking for the same thing, a man with money. He was a good-looking man, but he didn't have a lot of money. Now, this Douglas dude, he appeared to be loaded and Tommy didn't really know if that was something Sarah paid attention to or not. Still, it seemed she always hooked up with some guy every-time she came to vacation at the resort, and this time was no different. He burned with rage as he watched Sarah lead Douglas into the apartment.

Sarah showed Douglas straight to the bedroom, she was a no-nonsense, why-wait-kinda-girl, and Douglas certainly didn't have a problem with that. True to herself, Sarah pulled her top straight over her head as soon as she stepped inside. She enjoyed watching Douglas's jaw drop to the floor with her clothes. She took his breath away as she lay back sprawled on the bed. He gazed down at her with a longing and desire he hadn't felt in a long time. He couldn't wait to get his hands on her.

She smiled up at him as she crawled on to the bed and on top of him. Still fully clothed, she gave him an encouraging smile as he stared at her in wonder. She reached for his shirt and yanked it straight over his head, and moved swiftly down to relieve him of his pants. Douglas was naked on his hands and knees over her in a flash; he could hardly believe his luck. He leant down, gave her a tantalizing full kiss on the lips, and felt her wrap her arms around him. Sarah felt shock waves pulse through her entire body, awakening her desire for him even further. Impatient to realize what she had let herself in for, she slid down underneath Douglas to come face to face with his massive throbbing member.

His cock was huge, and as it slid into her mouth, it nearly choked her with its girth. When he made his initial move, his hands held her head to his cock, encouraging her to move up and down on it. She savored the taste of him, one of manliness and a woody, musky odor. She teased his balls with her fingers, stroking them back and forth as her mouth curled around him, sliding to the very tip and then coming all the way back down, hard and fast. She could feel him inhale sharply as she sucked at the ridge of flesh just under his dick.

"God," he moaned, closing his eyes as he reveled in the feeling of her mouth on his cock. "You're really good at that." She wanted him so desperately, wanted to feel his dick entering her. She was thinking about it so hard that her legs parted wide as she sucked him. He noticed, and with her clothes gone, he was able to easily move his fingers down to her pussy to finger her. He found her clit first, swollen and hard.

"Damn, you want me bad don't you? It's okay baby, I'm going to fuck you like you've never been fucked. You're going to love my cock in your pussy. In fact, maybe I'll let you have me right now." He pulled his dick out of her mouth, allowed her to stroke on him a few times and then turned her over, making her get on her hands and knees. "You have a nice tight ass too. I'd love to fuck your ass, mmmm... Damn, you are delectable."

His words were making her hornier by the minute, and when she felt the head of his cock right there at her pussy, she pushed back hard on him, sending him ramming into her wetness full and deep. She cried out in pleasure, his cock filling her pussy completely, just like she'd known he would. When he began moving he seemed to hit every nerve, and he was rubbing directly against her g-spot with every thrust. She pushed back on him, meeting him thrust for thrust, becoming wetter with excitement with every hardened push back in her. At one point, she stopped him, rising to her knees and squeezing him hard inside of her. She used his legs for support as she moved herself up and down on top of his dick. She could feel his cum seeping out, so she moved much faster, her nails biting into his thighs. The harder he hit into her the more she wanted it. She didn't think it was forceful enough. She loved the hard, fast, deep strokes. Those were the ones that made her cum like crazy.

As she continued to ride him, she couldn't believe that only after a few hours of talking they were already fucking like animals. She didn't care though, she'd needed someone to fill a void and he'd been there. Still, looking back, it had been way too easy....

9 OCEAN'S EDGE 2

Ménage

Sarah was as quiet as possible as she moved away from Douglas. He was sleeping like a mere babe, all curled up and comfy like, with a smile still present on his face. She had no intention of waking him up, though he was going to have to leave very soon. Staring at him lying in her bed sleeping as he was, she had no idea what had possessed her to fuck him. He wasn't the type of man that made her happy, but he was a good roll in the hay, she couldn't deny that one. She thought about touching him but decided against it. It was best to leave things as they were.

The sun was beginning to set in the sky. Sarah loved to go out in the evening, with the cool ocean breeze against her skin and the night's moon shining down upon her. She found it to be quite captivating herself. She could feel it calling to her, urging her to leave the lonely confines of her lodgings and run amongst the darkened clouds building in the sky.

Slipping her feet into her sandals and grabbing her shawl, she headed for the front door, anxious for escape from it all. She glanced back at Douglas, hoping he would be gone when she returned. In that instant she realized she didn't want to see him again. It had been a onetime affair.

Once she opened the door, she realized she didn't need the silk scarf around her shoulders at all; the humidity ran into her like a steam train in that second. While it had cooled off dramatically on the island, there certainly was a heavy haze in the evening air. She made her way down the walkway, passing other tourists as she went and some Islanders as well. Many of the faces were all familiar to her and brought her a little bit of contentment.

Just a few feet down she heard Douglas call out from in behind her and putting her hand up to her brow she saw him standing halfway down the long hill up to the complex, waving at her. She waved back but instead of him heading toward her general direction, he veered off to the left and disappeared out of sight. It was just as well really; out of sight out of mind. That was how she saw it. He really wasn't anything special. Sarah was fairly certain she would run into him again during her stay, but strangely enough, she found herself not looking forward to it. Instead, the image in her mind was Tommy.

She kept walking in the opposite direction,

going across the pier and outward to the water's edge. She wasn't really paying attention to how far she was walking either, not with the comfort that it was offering to her. She enjoyed the passersby and their conversations amongst one another, some of a romantic nature while others were just everyday talks. It was then that the loneliness filled her, reminding her of her own inadequacies and problems that remained unsolved. Sarah knew she was looking for all the answers in all the wrong places. When she thought of Tommy, she knew good and well he wasn't a solution. There was something different about him that hinted of hope. She'd never considered it before, perhaps because she'd been afraid to. She sighed deeply, wondering, just wondering what could happen?

She'd known him for such a long time and they'd always hung out. He'd always been the type to make her feel better about just anything that was bothering her. She needed him then, not so much for sex, as they'd never thought about that...well at least she hadn't, but for comfort and support. Sarah had just given herself to a man she didn't know the first thing about, and while she'd enjoyed it, she knew what it looked like. She didn't want to be that type of woman. Only those closest to her knew what she was really like and what she was really all about.

Walking along the water's edge, lost in her thoughts she didn't hear the voice calling out to her at first. It wasn't until she'd passed the tiki bar where Tommy worked that she looked up, realizing how far down the beach she'd walked. When she was preparing to turn around and begin walking back, he was there. His shadow showed up under the moonlight, just a few inches from hers. Her breath caught in her throat. They didn't speak. It was in silence that he slid his arm about her shoulders, and it was only then she was brave enough to look at him...Tommy.

"Oh Tommy, I can always count on you can't I? How is it you always know where I'm going to be when I'm here?" He tightened his grip about her but was in no way going to tell her how he knew. Sometimes he followed her. Sometimes he just had the intuition to know where to look. He smiled at her, leaning in to her and bringing her closer to his chest as he felt her sigh.

"Oh Sarah...Sarah, you just are so lost aren't you. Why do you look for the things you need in all the wrong places?" She dared to look him in the eyes and saw his open honesty and the concern mirrored there for her. She stopped walking and turned in his arms.

"Tommy, do you think me a whore, a slut? Sometimes...sometimes, I feel that is what I am. I look so long and hard for love, someone to care for me the way I used to be cared for. I don't know what I'm thinking." He held her to him, holding his breath. It was the first time that they'd ever been so close to intimacy before and he found himself enjoying every second, the smell of her...he could almost taste her sweetness in his mouth.

Tommy almost hated himself for thinking of

having her during a time of such struggle in her life but he was just a man after all. Her womanly form pressed so hard into him was slowly arousing his senses to a burning inferno, one that he wanted to have satiated. He could feel her body heat coming through her clothing, as thin as it was. It was the only thing separating them from skin to skin contacts, but his cock was still growing bigger in his pants. He didn't know if she could feel it pressing into her abdomen or not, but oh how he wanted to grind it against her. When she looked up at him, he couldn't hold back. His lips slowly began descending to hers and surprisingly, she didn't pull away.

She didn't respond initially, but when his hand came to the side of her face, the longing that she needed, the desire that she craved all came down upon her with the feel of his utter sincerity. She responded back, her tongue moving inside his mouth and tangling with his. It was then that she could feel his manhood pulsating against her. She couldn't stop from realizing his girth, having never noticed it before.

Tommy pulled her away from the moonlight and away from the water's edge, more toward the overpass of the bridge, and then under it, away from eyes that might see them. Pressing her back against the cold slab of hard concrete, he did grind himself into her sweetness, hard and with intent. His breath was coming in gasps. The fact that she had given herself to another man that very afternoon didn't stop him. He wanted to erase that face from her mind, to show her true devotion, not just a fucking.

He slowly removed her clothing, allowing his knuckles to run against her already hard nipples and enjoying her moans of delight. Sometimes his name slipped past her lips, and others she simply begged him to take her, to fill her with his hardness. He didn't unbutton her pants but rather ripped them free, busting the zipper off the material and allowing him to slip his hand down to her pussy beneath the material. He wasn't surprised to find she wore no panties. He found her to be so wet for him; he could only imagine dropping to his knees and sucking at her pussy right then and there.

Jerking her pants down to her ankles, she kicked her feet from them as he removed her bra from her breasts. Fully exposed to his ravaging gaze, now she wanted him, reached for him, but he didn't let her touch him. He stripped slowly, watching her eyes take him in, his huge cock springing forth to graze against her hand. He was well endowed, and rippling with muscle. She couldn't imagine why she had never noticed him before. Now, she was aching for him, and not just for his cock but his caress, his words of devotion...

Sarah didn't hesitate to go to him as he stood naked before her. She gyrated against him, and him being taller than she was, she found it disappointing to not make the contact with his manhood that she wanted. He could sense it and bent to kiss her, lowering him so he could make contact where she wanted it. She stroked him, teasing his balls at the same time and whispering in his ear. She could tell he liked it; but she wanted this to be good for him as it was their first time together. In it, all her worries dissipated as she became totally focused on him and his pleasuring her.

"Tommy, Tommy...don't tease me; why do you do this to me?" He swallowed her words with his mouth, sucking at her tongue as he plunged his finger into her wet slit. Deeper he moved, enacting what he wanted to do when he did enter her. Moving his tongue from her mouth to her breasts, he suckled her nipples like a babe, stretching them out and encouraging them to become much harder. She arched up into him, cumming into his hand in a squirting orgasm as she cried out his name, her lashes moist with tears of happiness.

Tommy was near pain with his cock now rigidly hard, pointed against her, but still he didn't plunge into her like he wanted. He wanted to imagine the warmth of her mouth to be that of her pussy as she slid down him and took his dick in, sucking him slowly and surely. He was much too big to take all the way but she enjoyed pleasuring his head, sucking intently on the ridge of skin that rose gently underneath. When he pulled her back up, claiming her mouth again, the head of him ran in between her lips, sometimes entering her just a little before withdrawing.

"Do you really want this Sarah? Do you really want me or is this just another way to try and relieve yourself of your own burdens?" She stared at him wide eyed, waiting for him to take her, wanting it, but in shock at the same time. Her pussy was nearly moaning for him, like a hungry belly.

"Yes, I want you Tommy. You! I don't know why it has taken me so long to realize this, but please, please don't make me beg." She kissed him hard, encouraging him as best she could to take her by opening her legs wide and allowing him to enter her when he wanted.

"I'm going to fuck you Sarah, fuck you like you've never been fucked before. You won't think of anyone else, I promise you." As he grabbed his own cock and stroked himself for one second, he rubbed himself between her slit hard, pushing in and out, all the while loving how her muscles sucked at him and left him wet with her juices. When he finally thrusted his dick in her he went all the way, up to the hilt of his staff, buried deep inside of her sweet pearl of pleasure. She screamed out his name for how large he was and how tight her pussy felt around him.

"Oh Tommy, fuck me! I want you too..." Her pleading egged him on, and he couldn't stop, driving his manhood deeper into her. Each time he held himself at the very edge of her entrance, and every thrust he rammed harder into her, feeling the very edge of her uterus as he moved. Her juices spilled out onto his cock, dripping from her pussy in excitement as she came again and again.

He couldn't hold back any longer with her tightness encircling him. It was pure heaven as he felt himself sliding easily in and out of her, her muscles gripping him with each individual thrust. When he exploded his seed inside of her, he could feel her nails biting into his buttocks, pulling him in as deeply as her body would allow. She wrapped her thighs around him, sucking hard at his cock with her muscles in a vice like motion.

Finally spent, yet not wanting to withdraw he rolled over, having her now positioned on top of him where their eyes could meet with him still pulsating in her. She smiled at him, rubbing his face and caressing his chest with her lips at times. She couldn't tell him she loved him, though she knew that is what he longed to hear. Sarah did know that she wanted more from him than just sex. She did have feelings for him and knew that they went back farther than just that evening. Laying her body across his she closed her eyes, feeling his heart beating beneath her ear.

"Tommy you have to be the most unique of men. I don't think I ever could have dreamed this is what it would be like to be with you." He smiled to himself, caressing her hair with his fingers. He could feel the slowing of her own heartbeat, the contentment easing from her as they lay there together. Nothing could have been more perfect in that moment, it all felt right. Sarah had never felt more appreciated in any man's arms than in his. He was so perfect, too perfect really. She worried that he would somehow disappear from her sight. Her worries manifested in words, but she didn't mean to say them. It was too late.

"Tommy, don't ever leave me, ever." He whispered back to her, running his fingers in a gentle caress across her shoulder blades and back.

"Never would I leave you. I love you Sarah, and always have been here for you." It was the perfect ending to their sexual tryst, the perfect beginning for their future together.

10 LOVE ME TENDER

Kayla loved the warmth of the morning sun, it remained steadfast as one of the most valuable times of her day and she never grew tired of it. With each passing evening, and the next early morning the sun seemed to bring about a different array of color among all the growing prairie flowers and silky green fern grasses. Even the milkweed, which grew in abundance around the farm, was somehow enlightened under those dewy rays.

The scene was simply beautiful, with the grazing of the horses in the distance and the sounds of the morning bringing in the bright new day. She lived for it because it energized her. More than anything else, Kayla loved the zestiness of life on the open plains and often she was more of a wanderer herself, slipping past the hands to the outer banks of the ranch for exploring. It was always John who found her though, and always him who she sought to be with.

A few of the workers were already up and preparing to mosey out to the farthest end of the ranch too, with John Straight Arrow always one of the earliest risers. She watched him often and couldn't stop herself from fantasizing about his sinewy brown skin pressed up against her own milky whiteness.

Kayla was young and naïve, but not stupid. She knew the ways of a man and a woman but she had yet to lie with anyone. Her father had long since passed away, dead from a very harsh winter three years past. He had developed a nagging cough that has just never gone away. She knew if he were alive, he wouldn't want her fawning over a dirty Indian. Even though John Straight Arrow had been with their ranch for quite some time, about 2 years in fact, her daddy would have had him shackled and whipped for looking twice at his daughter.

But twice he did, and even more than that. They'd been meeting secretly for some time, her mother unaware. Kayla sighed. Her mother was so far gone now...If it weren't for the day nurse on hand coming to look after her she would have been long dead too. Ever since her father's passing, things had changed. It had been Hughie who had gone to her mother and told her they needed more hands for the spring harvest coming. She had agreed.

Two years ago that had been...Two years she and John had been caring for one another secretly. Kayla felt it was time they came out of hiding though, despite what anyone would

think.   John had told her it would be a
mistake, that they would seek to lynch him for
loving a white woman, and one that was as
influential as her. She didn't see it that way.

There was many a time they'd lain in the
hay together, in the back of one of the barns
and talked about just running away together.
That was what she longed for.   It was the
perfect time to do so too, with spring's arrival
and life being renewed. It was also the perfect
time to finally get her own love consummated
while in his embrace.

He'd told her the only way they would
survive was to go with his people, return back
to the Cheyenne tribe that he had separated
from so long ago. He had told her why he'd
left before, but she sometimes forgot, her mind
focused on more important details of their
relationship. He must have felt her eyes upon
him because they met across the distance.
The sun had risen higher in the sky and his
dark hair held that hint of blue low-light color
to it. As the wind struggled to lift some of the
loose sacks of the ground by his feet his hair
blew back across his shoulders, toying with
her emotions.

Transfixed as she was she didn't hear Kyle
approach her, and when his hand fell to her
shoulder, she jumped about half an inch from
the ground, her hand splaying across her
chest as if to slow her racing heart. They both
laughed   lightly   and   he   apologized   for
frightening her the way he did.

"You must have been really focused there
Miss Kayla. I'm sorry for alarming you but
your momma is lookin' for you." She nodded

as she eased by him, but her caught her by the edge of her elbow before she could finish scurrying away.

He was a broad framed man, much older than John, and certainly about 20 years her senior. She knew what he wanted but it wasn't anything she was interested in. It was common for men on the plains to take younger brides, basically because they knew that they weren't barren and would be guaranteed sons to take over their places when they were gone. It wasn't something that Kayla wanted at all.

She knew that Kyle had an awareness of her current state, and being that she was in charge of the ranch with her mother being so incapacitated, he couldn't demand anything from her unless he wanted a lashing himself. That wasn't a philosophy that she lived by though and she certainly wasn't going to have him flogged for his abrasive actions when he didn't mean anything by them.

"Kyle, kindly let go of my arm." He hesitated before finally doing so, but his eyes were condemning. He cleared his throat before speaking to her. She didn't know if it was so he wouldn't sound so harsh, or because he just had something caught there.

"Kayla, you know your momma needs you to set a plan for a decent life and she thinks that I would be the best suitor for you. You know that." She turned to him, her eyes blazing with anger at his words. He normally was very quiet and didn't speak out, but she supposed her mother had encouraged this action.

"Just who do you think you are, trying to control me and tell me what I should and shouldn't do? You're way too old for me and I won't have anything to do with this, I'm telling you now." She spun away from him on that note, something that John Straight Arrow noticed as well. He seemed as if he were going to approach the two of them but she waved him away.

"Kyle, no one tells me how to live my life or who to share it with. I think I've made it clear enough who has my attentions on this ranch, now, if you'll excuse me I'll go and tell my momma the same thing." He didn't stop her, didn't protest, and when he turned seeing John's eyes on him in the harshest of ways he knew to certainly back down. He wasn't that stupid.

Kyle glanced back to where Kayla had disappeared off too one time, but after that he turned his attention to getting the hands ready to head out to the farthest west bank. Some of the cattle had gotten out of the fencing and they had to go and corral them, a chore which could take all day if they didn't do it right. John decided to stay to mend some of the shoes in the barn, hoping that Kayla would come looking for him later.

She didn't look well, lying there in her bundle of sleeping skirts, her hair spread out across the pillow. No, her mother had aged quite a bit, and after their conversation of what life would be best for her, Kayla felt guilty. She worried that she had caused her mother to become overexerted, leading to her becoming weaker. The nurse had told her that wasn't the case but she stayed for a little while anyway. Seeing that she wasn't going to wake up anytime soon, her thoughts turned to John. She needed him so desperately in that moment.

Kayla had always tried to make others happy, never thinking about her own needs but she had grown tired of that, especially now with her daddy dead and gone, and her mother soon to follow. Life was too short for living for someone else and she was ready to make that move to John, to change everything. They didn't have to run away if they didn't want too, but they could. She didn't care where they were as long as they were together.

She spoke to the woman tending her mother and told her to let her know if there was any change before she headed off into the direction of the barn where she knew John was waiting for her. She could feel him there as she drew closer. The soft whinny of one of the horses caused her to look in that direction as her eyes adjusted to the dimming light within. She saw him at the longest end, working with the shoes that had been damaged. He was good at that kind of thing, things that called for his hands.

She couldn't help but think of those hands against her skin, raising her skirts and touching her in the sweetest of places. It was what she had been dreaming of for so very long. Kayla didn't care if their first time was in a barn or in a soft bed, she simply couldn't wait for him any longer. His back was to her and her steps so light he didn't hear her approach. He probably smelled her perfume though because as she came right upon him he raised his head.

John stood, knowing that she was there in behind him, smelling her even. His heart thudded heavily in his chest as he could sense what she wanted, what they both wanted. He turned slowly, surprised at what he saw. She was looking down, unbuttoning each button on the bodice of her gown, slowly, and with steady precision. When his darker hand covered her own she stopped, her breath catching in her throat at the needy gaze that was in his eyes.

"Let me do this Kayla. Let me." She all but fell into him, her mouth coming into his own and her lips parting for his seeking tongue as he reached beneath her body to her bare skin. He could feel her nipples behind her shift, hard, erect, and dying for his mouth and tongue. His own desire was building, becoming so hard that he could barely see straight. He could only think of himself there, inside of her, taking her and claiming her as his own.

"I want you John Straight Arrow. I want you to pleasure me as I've wanted for so very long, to be your woman, and only your woman. Let me feel you fill me." He smothered her words with a deeply prolonged kiss, pressing himself against her as hard as he could. Her skirts were whisked away, falling to the barn floor and becoming a blanket for them to fall upon.

Each time their eyes met and held the passion just grew stronger between them.

They passed words, words that they had kept inside for quite a while. They were things that needed to be said, like laundry that needed a clean breeze. It allowed them to feel free to love one another. When they were finally both naked, lying there together, his cock pressed against one of her thighs, they simply caressed each other like two newborn strangers. Enjoying the seconds and relishing in the moment.

It no longer mattered to either of them whether the townsfolk accepted their relationship or not. It didn't matter what the ranch hands would think. Kayla already knew what she'd say to any one of them if they commented in the wrong way. There were always more hands to hire, and while these had been with her family for a while, it wouldn't change anything. Just because John was an Indian meant nothing, he was a good man. That was all that mattered to her.

Soon, as he continued to touch her, taking his time to kiss and arouse her even more her thoughts of concern fled her mind. He was the center of everything and when she reached her hand down to stroke his hard length, enjoying the silky smoothness of him, she was certainly gone to all of the concerns. She wanted him to fill her with his seed, allow her to give him children, and make his life complete the way he did for her.

When he entered her, it was with one long thrust, and with slight hesitation until she adjusted to him. She moved first, accepting his girth and welcoming it, allowing him to let go and take her with the abandon he really wanted too. Each move sent a moan pouring from her lips, one louder than the next, encouraging him to go deeper within her and to touch that very precipice that would have her spilling her sweet juices all over him.

Time stood still as their bodies moved against one another, sometimes her taking the position upon him. She'd never ridden atop anything like she was now, and Kayla was finding she liked being in the saddle, straddling him and controlling his cock inside of her wet slit as she was. She hovered above him at times, her muscles squeezing around him before she allowed her body to slide back down his hard member.

When John could take her teasing torment no longer, he pushed her back to the earthen floor, pounding into her like a mad man until she felt him begin to quiver and stiffen, throwing his head back in great need. She could feel his seed flooding into her. Grasping his hips, she pulled him forward deeper, and wrapped her thighs about his waist holding him there hard. She whispered to him,

"Perhaps we shall create a child in this darkened barn today John Straight Arrow. Maybe a little girl with dark curly hair or a little boy with the dark eyes like yourself?" Her words comforted him as he fell against her, balancing some of his weight on his forearms before rolling to the side, staying inside of her as well. He kissed her before pulling her towards his chest and nestling her body up against his own.

"Perhaps a child will take root in your body from our love making Kayla, but then so will many more in time. I will never get enough of you, and the more children we have the better our lives will be filled." She smiled, her heart thumping in rhythm with his own, finally feeling at peace with the choice that she had made.

She kept telling herself that it wasn't wrong; it was the right thing to do. They deserved the chance, and certainly she did. Their lives could be vivacious, and their children's lives could be extravagantly rich and emboldened. That was what she wanted, something unique, something inspiring. It was certainly what she was going to get too!

11 WHEN BLOOD RUNS DEEP

Charisse sat quietly in her father's office. She stared cross-eyed at her bangs that curled down to just above her delicate eyebrows. They were stuck together in the middle, creating an ugly part that was driving her insane. She curled her sinfully full lips and gently puffed a breath at them, hoping to unstick them without the need for actual physical labor.

She had always been a well-protected girl, spoiled rotten some would say. Still, Charisse felt that she'd never had a chance to really live, not yet. There was a deep yearning inside of her, something she just couldn't explain, and some nights she would lay in her bed simply fighting the urge to run away and abandon everything she'd ever known. It was a feeling she just didn't like. What was worse was when she tried to talk to her father about out he avoided the issues. It appeared to her that there was just some deep dark secret lying between them. Sometimes it was so heavy she felt she couldn't even breathe. Looking at her bangs now, in the reflection of her phone, she gave up...

She sighed in defeat and let her eyes roam through the lavishly decorated room. Charisse never understood her father's obsession with tarnished brass and bronze. The office would have looked much more luxurious with a few pieces of sparkling silver strewn here and there. She felt somber from just sitting there.

Her mind drifted away from her musings about her father's décor. She thought about the dream she had last night, which was nearly identical to the dream from the night before, and a hundred before that. Charisse's chest tightened ever so slightly.

In her dreams, Charisse would be in the throes of passion, where she was making love to a handsome, strapping man or alone, playing out a fantasy while caressing her undulating body. Once she was sitting on a sparse mountainside, gazing up at the moon as it hung high in the night sky. Just as she was approaching her moment of bliss or contentment, something evil and malevolent would rip her from the edge.

Sometimes it was Charisse's father. Sometimes it was some dark, hideous beast, hidden in the shadows. All she could ever see were its bright, hungry eyes, burning through the darkness and into her soul. She didn't know what it meant. Maybe that is how she really saw her father; she didn't know.

A side door opened and two large men

dragged a third, babbling and sobbing, by his shoulders. His feet slid across the deep, rich color of the expensive, wooden floor. After they disappeared around the corner of the hall, her father emerged through the doorway. He smiled and offered her his arms as he moved effortlessly toward her.

"Ah, Charisse, my daughter," he said, accepting her embrace with the love only a father can give to his only child.

"Another satisfied customer I see?" she smiled and slid into the chair across from his desk again.

Her father pursed his lips slightly and answered with a nod before sinking into the lavish, leather, high-back chair behind his desk. Charisse never pretended she didn't know what her father did, even if it did make her sick to her stomach from time to time. How could she be critical of him when his illegal endeavors provided so much comfort in her style of living?

Frankie Fazliani, better known as Frankie the Faz or Frankie the Fish, was the Boss of one of New York's most sinister, iron-fisted Mob rings. He was your classic "bust heads now, ask questions later" type of wiseguy. Frankie was cold and calculating, vicious and ruthless, and so completely fearless that once he had his thugs wipe out an entire rival family just because his daughter was not invited to a birthday party. That was the man sitting across from Charisse right now.

Father and Daughter exchanged small talk and Frankie made a bid to get his daughter more involved with the family business.

Granted he intended on living forever, he wasn't as young as he used to be, and every new day was a bullet waiting to end his reign. He wanted her to run the show when he was gone but Charisse didn't show much interest in it.

"Good night dad," she said, leaning over to give him a peck on the cheek before heading off for the night.

Frankie rubbed his eyes and watched her leave. He traced his tongue along the edge of his teeth and wondered if she would ever be like him. Under different circumstances, he'd be fine with her not wanting to run the family business, but she was his daughter after all. It was in her blood to follow in his footsteps.

Charisse flashed a wink at the seedy-looking henchman that guarded her apartment door. She thought it was cute how her father was so over-protective but she was well aware of his motivation to have such ways. It wasn't like Frankie didn't own the top three floors of the tower. Charisse didn't get as much as a blink from the guy. She gave her long, raven hair a sensuous flip as she passed and closed the door behind her.

After discarding her clothes and pulling on just a black, silk robe before getting into the shower, Charisse walked into the kitchen to pour a glass of wine. She paused at the large windows and gazed out at the city skyline. New York City was nothing short of stunning at night. Her sparkling eyes lifted from the city to the unusually bright, full moon.

She could almost see every nook and cranny of its surface. It was beautiful and hung nestled gently between a million pinpoints of light. Charisse felt herself drawn to it as if it called to her like a lover. Her large brown eyes followed every contour and she felt her chest rise and fall deeply with each passing moment.

"Where are you?" she whispered then felt a familiar tingle dance up her spine.

Charisse pressed her hand against the glass and caressed the outline of the moon while she brushed the back of her hand down her neck and between her large, pillowy breasts. The touch of her hand through the silk forced her eyes closed for a moment. There were so many things in her life that she hadn't experienced because of who her father was. Being with a man was one of them.

There were no dates, no handsome man holding her hand while walking through the park, no love or lust. It was only her and her father and his goons. She desired to be held and loved tenderly by a rugged, loving man. Perhaps she was just a romantic at heart, but she burned to give into the desire that boiled inside of her.

Charisse slowly untied her robe and let it drop from her shoulders. She stood there in all her naked glory, staring into eternity and wondering where her place was in the world and if she would really find love. She hated the fact that she'd spend another night alone, like the night before and the night before that.

She placed her hands on the window and pressed her soft breasts against its cool, smooth surface, feeling the heat of the night coursing through her body again, as it had every night for the past year. It was like a starving animal inside of her, clawing its way out in search of something to satisfy her cravings. She growled herself, in total frustration. Her insides felt like molten lava spooling through her veins. She ran her hands through her hair, not knowing where else to put them.

Even if Charisse couldn't find love then maybe lust would suffice. Lust. Pure, animalistic lust. She rubbed her breasts against the glass and ran her tongue along its surface. She felt the desire stirring deep inside of her, begging to be released. She moaned against the glass and ran her slender hands over her curvaceous, creamy ass. The musk of her overpowering arousal began to fill her pulsing nostrils.

It was the most intense craving she had felt in months and the inferno that burned deep in her succulent, virgin flower threatened to consume her. Slowly Charisse turned around and leaned against the cool glass. She covered an erect nipple with the palm of her hand and gently dug the tips of her fingers into her supple breast. Her other hand travelled across her smooth, flat stomach and inched toward the source of her heat.

Her hips moved gently and she squeezed her eyes shut when her fingers found her sensitive nub, partly nestled within her silky flesh. Charisse parted her creamy thighs gently and growled in need as she moved her fingers deftly between her moistening, womanly folds. She was so hot that she could have ravished the thug keeping watch outside of her door and there would have been no stopping her.

Maybe that was what she needed to satisfy her carnal cravings. Maybe she didn't need to make love to a life partner. Maybe she just needed a good fuck. As the fantasies swirled through her mind, she delicately pressed her fingers deep into her dripping wet flesh. She loved how it felt to pleasure itself, as it was like some innate ability she had been blessed with. She always knew exactly where to stroke to hit the right spot too. Her girlfriends always conceded to her that they did the same thing but were unable to orgasm themselves.

She supposed she was just one of those super sensitive women, the kind that needed a good pounding and enjoyed more touching than others. She could feel her pleasures building and she dove deeper, every time pulling away with more juices following in her fingers wake. She would have gotten the fake dildo that one of her girlfriends had bought for her as a joke, but she couldn't stop. She didn't want to.

"Mmmmm," she groaned as she added a second.

She eased her fingers in and out of her quickly and determinedly, pleasing her in the same fashion they had several times a week. Her hot pussy cried in agony as she pulled her fingers from inside and lifted them to her lips. Slowly she slid them into her mouth and moaned at the taste of her own juices. Finally, she pulled her saliva-soaked fingers from her wet mouth and took several deep breaths.

Charisse swallowed hard and scooped up

her robe before disappearing into her bedroom. Whatever it was that called to her like an anguished ghost had started a fire deep inside of her. She retired to her bedroom in hopes of fending off the creature but knew that eventually the animal in her would win out.

Two weeks passed and Charisse's father noticed her becoming more irritable and angry. Several times Frankie tried to sit her down and hunt for the root of her troubles, but each time she just blew him off. Today, however, he decided not to pry and looked at her with as loving eyes as he could.

"Gimme a sec," he told her then pulled out his cellphone.

Frankie mashed his thick, calloused fingers into his cellphone and waited impatiently. He remembered a time cellular phones didn't exist. It wasn't that technology evolved too fast for him. It just seemed that as things became more high-tech they became more cumbersome and prone to malfunction.

"Porky, it's Frankie," he said to the goon on the other end of the call.

"Take today off," Frankie ordered then thumbed the call off.

Charisse's eyes lit up. She couldn't believe it, and found herself in shock. Her father had called his goons off for once. Frankie nodded then pulled out a small pistol from his desk drawer. At first Charisse was going to resist but decided that if her father was going to call off the Goon Squad, she could at least make the compromise and it wasn't like she hadn't carried a gun before.

Frankie watched his daughter in complete silence as she took the pistol and tucked it away in her tiny purse. It was time to let her experience life without his constant protection. He trusted her and hoped she could protect herself. Time would tell whether or not his trust would be misplaced.

Hours later, Charisse basked in the afternoon sun as she waited patiently for him. Unbeknownst to her father, she had met a young man months ago. He was handsome and caring and most importantly, he didn't care that she was the daughter of a ruthless mob boss. They had only met a handful of times before. She didn't want to risk getting ratted out by her father's thugs, but this time the worry was gone.

But each time they met was more magical than the last. In her heart, she felt Donovan was different. So different than anyone she had ever met before that she swore he could be the one. And now with her looser reigns, she had the opportunity to explore their relationship.

"Charisse, mi amore," Donovan said, leaning down and placing a gentle kiss on her smooth, bare shoulder.

Charisse popped up from the park bench, wrapped her arms around him, and drew him in. Their lips met in furious passion. She pressed herself against him, feeling the firmness of his muscular chest against her through the sheer fabric of her dress. She needed him badly and hoped that Donovan could handle the storm of frustration she'd unleash upon him.

Hand-in-hand, Charisse and Donovan walked through Central Park on their way to his place. They talked a little here and there as they enjoyed each other's company. Donovan seemed a bit surprised when she told him how her father called off his thugs to let her actually have a life. He'd heard stories about Frankie and the mob boss didn't seem like the kind to let his daughter gallivant around without someone protecting her.

"Maybe he wants you to appreciate his protectiveness," Donovan said as they walked.

"I know. I understand where he's coming from," she replied. Her voice held a touch of contempt in it.

"I'm almost 23. I want him to know I can make good decisions and take care of myself," Charisse continued.

The truth was, she hadn't really thought of the consequences of not having her father's goons around watching over her. The desire to do what she wanted without her every move being reported back to Frankie had blinded her to the reality of her life as a mobster's child. But she was with Donovan now and she felt safer than she'd ever felt before.

"I'm sure you can handle yourself," he said with a mischievous wink then a little pat on her rear.

Charisse purred and nuzzled against him, growing impatient. She wondered if today would be the day Donovan took her. She'd been yearning for it since they'd met though she realized that back then it wasn't about being with Donovan, it was about satisfying her sexual frustration.

Now, however, it was different. She didn't look at Donovan and see slab of meat with a penis. She truly cared for him, maybe even loved him, and wasn't afraid to show him just how much either. Today, for the first time, the notion of her inexperience with men crept into her brain.

Charisse wasn't sure if it was that or the sweet excitement of anticipation. She watched plenty of pornographic videos over the years of having to satisfy her own urges and she had learned quite a bit from them. She was quite confident that she knew enough to satisfy Donovan. All she could do was wait and see.

Finally they were at his place, a meager apartment that looked very much like her father's office. It was quaint but dull. Charisse smiled politely and told him she loved it. Donovan returned her smile and eyed her slowly from head to toe. She could feel the desperate heat in his stare and resisted the urge to pounce on him and use him every which way she could.

She sat quietly on the couch and watched him pour some wine. It was complete and utter torture. Charisse had waited for so long for this moment and Donovan knew it. He purposely took his time. He wanted to tease her, to make her hotter until she was about to burst, then and only then would he take her to his bed. He wanted her to ache for him and only him.

Donovan knew she had never made love to a man before. He also knew of her deliciously dirty self-pleasuring sessions, how there were days she refused to get out of bed because she was so aroused that she couldn't keep her hands off her yearning, young body. He had spent many nights lying awake in bed, knowing she was home, covered in a light sheen of sweat, moaning in ecstasy as she fought to quell the hunger inside of her.

Donovan would close his eyes and imagine he was with her, plunging himself deep into her burning lust and then in that one powerful moment, he would climax with her. His seed would burst from his hard, throbbing manhood and splatter across his chiseled abs as he imagined filling her silky, moist depths with each lustful spurt.

Donovan glanced over at her on the couch as he corked the bottle of wine. The thought of it was arousing him now. His swollen length pressed against the fly of his jeans and begged to feel her warm, wet flesh around it.

When Donovan joined her on the couch, Charisse was waiting with the hungriest eyes he had ever seen. His growing bulge pulled her gaze to the front of his pants and teased her sensitive nipples to strain through her bra and the flimsy fabric of her sundress. She was done waiting.

Donovan handed her a glass of wine and watched her place it on the coffee table before sliding to her knees. She crawled fluidly toward him, like a cat stalking its prey. Donovan watched her with growing anticipation as she crawled between his knees. They both knew what was coming and Donovan simply leaned back against the couch and watched.

Charisse could feel the wetness of her panties brush the apex of her smooth, supple inner thighs. She stopped herself from reaching down and running her fingers over her sweet, burning folds like she had done a thousand times before. It was almost embarrassing that she was so used to pleasing herself that in the presence of Donovan, she automatically thought of her fingers instead of him.

After struggling against the raging inferno that burned inside of her, Charisse had Donovan's pants off and her fingers firmly wrapped around the girth of his shaft. She stared at his thick, pulsing manhood in amazement. She'd seen a hundred in her erotic movies and on the internet but she had never see one in real life, let alone touched one. Charisse began to tremble lightly as she nervously guided his swollen glans to her moist, pouting lips.

She nibbled on its spongy tip, teasing it with her lips and teeth before running her wet tongue along the tiny seam beneath. Donovan hissed in delight but made no move to urge her further. He wanted her to satisfy him at her own pace. Soon his swollen head slipped past her full, inviting lips as she sunk her juicy mouth down on his raging shaft.

Charisse moaned through her flaring nostrils as she worked his rock hard length in and out of her mouth, slowly at first then more furiously as her mouth relaxed further to take his size in. She didn't know how long he could handle it and left it up to him to stop her just short of reaching his peak, or not. Charisse was so enthralled with pleasing him that if he chose to fill her warm, wet mouth with his juice then she'd happily take every succulent drop.

She cupped and massaged his silky balls gently as she sucked his cock like an expert. Her fingers danced over his hard flesh as her lips travelled the length of his manhood. Having felt this day would come, she would practice with her dildo at home, perfecting her oral stimulation as she bided her time.

Donovan moaned and nearly dropped his glass of wine on the couch. He was expecting her to be reckless and full of energy but he'd never experienced a woman sucking him with such voracity as Charisse was. She took him fast and deep, shoving the excess of his pulsating meat down her eager, tightening throat. He literally drooled at the thought of her fucking him with the same sinful abandonment.

After just a few minutes of her adept pleasure, her jaw muscles began to ache. She let his swollen member pop from her tired mouth. It glistened with her saliva and pulsed in need. Seeing its subtle call for more stirred something inside of her, something powerful and animalistic.

Suddenly all of her wants and desires came crashing through her like a terrible thunderstorm of lust. All of her visions and fantasies of making love to Donovan twisted into something darker and more primitive. The wanton look in her eyes melted away from the pure, sizzling lust that threatened to burn Donovan to a crisp.

With a guttural growl, Charisse ripped open his shirt, shooting a myriad of defenseless buttons every which way. She clawed at his chiseled abs and ripped chest. She traced every curve of his powerful muscles and reveled in their tightness and strength. She tried to contain the blinding desire that welled up in her young, tender body.

She wanted to take it slow, she tried to, but she couldn't. The sexual beast inside of her had been awakened and demanded to be satisfied despite her fleeting self-control. Charisse dropped her dress to the floor and climbed onto him without removing her panties or bra. Charisse pulled her soaked, lacy thong to the side and guided Donovan's throbbing head to her warm, buttery folds.

Donovan held his breath and waited for the moment they had ached for so long. Charisse lowered herself and buried his rock hard length completely inside of her. She arched her smooth, contoured back and tilted her head, feeling herself completely filled by a man for the first time. She held her pose for several moments as she choked out several moans of desire.

Slowly she reached back and unclasped her bra, letting it fall onto Donovan's lap and freeing her ample, round breasts to him. Her hands slid up her smooth, flat stomach then cupped and squeezed her pillowy breasts. She felt her taut, sensitive nipples pressing hard against her palms as she dug her fingers roughly into her soft flesh.

After an eternity, Charisse dropped against Donovan. She pressed her hot tits against his powerfully muscled chest and kissed him deeply. Their moist tongues swirled hungrily together through the heat of their sinful desire. Donovan moved his strong hands down her creamy, smooth back and over her soft, round ass.

Charisse's head spun from the euphoria of their lust and when Donovan's powerful fingers dug into her fleshy cheeks, she howled into his mouth as her intense hunger took over. She started pounding her hips desperately against his lap. Charisse's body writhed wildly against Donovan as she drove his cock into her starving pussy like a wrecking ball.

Donovan thrust his hips to meet her movements. She moved like an insatiable animal, wild and reckless, free from her father's bonds, and intent on quenching the abyssal thirst she had harbored her entire life. Donovan's world fell away into darkness, leaving just them, alone, fucking vehemently on the couch.

Their powerful, lusting moans echoed through Donovan's apartment. He had surely bitten off more than he could chew. He expected hours of lovemaking, tender and tedious while they explored each other slowly, surely not the carnal heat threatening to ignite the entire building. He wasn't complaining.

His hands slid from her supple skin and dug into the couch's cushions. His knuckles strained white as he held on for his life as

Charisse reared back and started impaling herself even harder on his angry meat. She wailed hauntingly and her eyes rolled back into her head as she felt the deep, intense pang of her orgasm racing to the rim of her being. Then it hit her.

Her bursting pussy clenched around Donovan's cock like a terrible vice. It gripped his throbbing shaft and milked him hard and fast, begging it to erupt deep inside of her and add his crescendo to hers. Donovan tried to hold back for as long as he could but the slick, tight pumping of her ravenous grip dragged him over the edge with her.

Charisse growled at the top of her lungs as she rode the crest of her orgasm and felt Donovan's steaming, thick juices explode deep inside of her, flooding her quivering quim with every drop she could milk. Every desire she had ever felt, every fantasy she had ever imagined, every wish she had ever made came crashing down on them in a moment of blissful heat and launched them beyond the clouds.

They collapsed together in a tangle of flesh and gasps. Charisse trembled in Donovan's cradling arms as she fought to recover from the most powerful experience of her life. She nuzzled her face into the nape of his neck and submitted to her sudden fatigue.

As he tenderly stroked her sweaty cheek, Donovan wondered what he had gotten himself into or even more so, what he had gotten Charisse into. Frankly, he never expected this day to come and hadn't considered the repercussions. She was a part of his life now and he struggled inside as to whether or not tell her who he really was.

The next morning, Frankie pounded on his daughter's apartment door. Charisse groaned and rolled over in bed then cracked her heavy eyelids to glare at the clock. The red LEDs said 9:17 AM, not late but not too early, and yet it seemed like hours earlier than it really was. She hadn't come home until well after midnight, and two more sessions of heat and passion with Donovan had bled her strength.

Even though her lust seemed sated, she had the dream again. She stood before a wall of darkness and tried to peer beyond its surface. There was nothing, nothing at all. Then those eyes, those bright, burning eyes, appeared and struck her with excruciating fear and intense wonder. She could hear the beast's labored, ragged breath as it hungered for something.

Charisse turned and ran, trying to escape the void that moved as swiftly as she. She felt something tear across the hem of her flowing skirt. She looked back in terror and caught a glimpse of a hideous claw retreating into the pitch that followed her. It was disturbing, very disturbing. But it was morning now and the beast was gone. Despite her best efforts to ignore her father, she rolled over and groaned.

"Charisse!" Frankie growled from the other side of the door.

He waited patiently for his daughter to answer. In the entire world, only she could get away with making him wait. Anyone else would have had their door bashed in and their life stolen for the sake of Frankie's impatience.

"What?" Charisse said sleepily as she opened the door.

"Get dressed and come to my office now," he said angrily. "It's time you decide once and for all if you are in or not."

Charisse watched her father stalk away and frowned. She knew this day would come and wasn't sure if she could handle it or if she wanted to. She slipped on a pair of sweats and a tank top, tied her long hair into a messy ponytail, and left. The thoughts of Donovan that lingered in her head gave way to dread and wonder. Charisse held her breath as she entered her father's office and opened the door to his conference room.

She was greeted by a man gagged and strapped to a chair. His wild eyes bulged in pain and begged her to help him. His fear was rank and thick on her tongue and Charisse's stomach threatened to turn. She could hear his heart pounding a million times a second.

Frankie met his daughter with a kiss on the cheek. She eyed the hammer in his hand dubiously and connected the dots. The poor fellow's hand was strapped a piece of wood attached to the arm of the chair. He tried to curl his fingers beneath the pressure and shook his head violently.

"Charisse will teach you your first lesson," Frankie said to the bawling man and extended the handle of the hammer to his daughter.

"What lesson?" she asked. She knew the power she held over her father. There were a handful of family members who could get away with that question. She was one of them and the only one there.

"Little Mike here needs to be reminded of his place within the organization," Frankie said, not seeing the need to explain further, even to his own daughter.

"Remind him, will ya?" Frankie nodded to the hammer in his hand.

Charisse curled her fingers around the wooden handle. Her nostrils flared as she watched Little Mike squirm against his bonds. He looked familiar, but couldn't place his face. As the hammer fell, she remembered. He lived in Donovan's apartment building.

The hammer smashed into his pinky finger. Little Mike's eyes nearly popped out and he screamed into the gag.

"You follow my orders, you see," Frankie spat at him and nodded to Charisse.

She crushed the hammer into his ring finger. Little Mike screamed in agony. The hideous snap of his bones echoed through Charisse's ears. Her chest heaved with the power that suddenly overtook her body. There was a dark satisfaction in torturing this poor fellow for whatever transgression he made against her father.

Her father started to speak but Little Mike's muffled wailing cut him off as Charisse swung the hammer with both hands and obliterated his middle finger. Blood splattered across the wooden plank and she could smell the pain that screamed through the thug's body.

"You like that?" Charisse growled and pushed the bloody head of the hammer under Little Mike's chin. She peered into his eyes with venom and contempt. Something was taking its hold on her, pushing her to embrace the darkness hidden inside of her.

Suddenly those eyes flooded her mind again. She reeled at the satisfaction that burned so brightly from those eyes that she closed her own. Her chest heaved in shock as the image in her mind zoomed out and she finally saw the beast face to face. It was her.

She was naked. Blood covered her mouth and cheeks and trickled in long sinuous lines down her body. Her fingers were hideously crooked with long, thick nails that dripped blood too. Her image simply smiled at her with a nod.

Frankie stood by silently with his arms folded across his chest, watching Charisse come into her own as a member of their ring and more importantly, as his daughter. He glanced to the thug guarding the door. The bulky man arched a brow and nodded his approval slowly. They were all happily caught off guard by Charisse's sudden flavor for violence.

"You gonna cross my father again?" she asked darkly.

Little Mike whimpered uncontrollably and shook his head. His eyes begged her to believe him. The power of his fear drove the truth of his confession into her chest like a rough wooden spike. She believed him. Charisse nodded and started to withdraw, satisfied with the torture she put Little Mike through.

Almost satisfied, she crushed his index finger with the hammer uncontrollably, several times until his digit looked like ground meat. When she was done, Charisse smiled sweetly to her father. Now she was satisfied and tossed the hammer onto a small table in the corner. She kissed her father on the cheek and asked him to join her for breakfast in her apartment when he was finished.

Frankie nodded with a proud smile and watched his daughter go. He sensed something in her, something dark and malicious, burning to come to light. He thought it was time to reveal his darkest secret, one he had harbored her entire life. Breakfast seemed like the perfect opportunity.

Charisse sat curled up on her couch and silently stared at the moon. The shock of her father's words from breakfast haunted her. She had always felt something was different about her but she refused to believe what her father had confessed.

For the first time in a long time, she was able to look at the moon without the intense draw of lust that usually ended with her masturbating long and hard to appease her hunger. Did she subconsciously accept her father's admission and satisfy the beast within or was it that she was so distracted that she didn't notice it? Charisse couldn't decide.

She absently picked up a tiny vanity mirror and looked at herself. Charisse rolled her head from side to side and bared her teeth. They looked normal enough. None were more elongated or sharper than the others. If what Frankie had told her really was true, why hadn't she ever seen him as what he really was? She needed to go out then nabbed her cell phone to call Donovan.

"What's wrong?" he asked. She never called him at night.

"I'll explain when I see you. I just need to be somewhere besides here," she replied.

Donovan gave her a corner to meet him at. Although Frankie had given her a bit more freedom than before, they weren't ready to be seen together too close to Charisse's apartment building. Charisse tugged on her heavy trench coat over her t-shirt and sweats and left her apartment to meet with Donovan.

It took her a block or so before she realized what she was wearing and the absence of anticipation for meeting with the man that had so quickly took her heart. Charisse's lips bent into a frown. She should have gotten dressed up in something sexy for her man. Her tight, lavender dress would have been nice. It left most of her back exposed and she normally loved the way the stretchy fabric hugged her large breasts and round hips.

Today she was just out of it. Certainly distracted by what her father had admitted to her, Charisse found herself free of her usual routine. It bothered her somewhat and wondered if this is how it would be. She desperately hoped Donovan would understand and offer some words of comfort.

"Hey," Donovan said as he strolled up to her on the corner.

"Hey," she said distractingly.

"You okay? What's up?"

Charisse forced a smile and looped her arm in Donovan's. They walked without any particular destination in mind as she told him about breakfast with her father. Donovan listened intently but offered nothing in response and that irritated her a little.

When she was done with her story, Donovan simply kissed her on the top of the head and walked silently beside her. They crossed a few streets and meandered down a few alleys as if they were going somewhere now. Charisse didn't care where they were going. She felt safe with Donovan even if he wasn't giving her the response she desired.

As they approached a corner, the deep thrust of music touched Charisse's body and vibrated through her chest. She lifted her head from Donovan's arm and looked up at him. He smiled.

"I think it's what you need," he said.

"I'm not in the mood to club," she protested lightly.

"Trust me, okay?"

She did. Donovan led her around the corner then one more after that before stopping at what looked like a run-down, vacant apartment or office building. The music was coming from deep inside of the structure and there were no visible signs to indicate a name of the place.

A large, burly man opened a door to allow them to pass. Once inside, the music was deafening. The constant boom-boom assaulted Charisse's ears and pounded through her head. Donovan led her through a series of hallways and stairwells then finally out onto a small balcony that overlooked the dance floor.

"What is this place?" Charisse asked him.

"It's the place you need to be," he answered cryptically then looked at his watch. "We're just in time too."

Charisse looked at her own watch. It was a

few minutes before 1:00 AM. She counted the seconds with her watch and when it turned one, the music stopped, leaving a loud ring echoing through her ears.

"You know what time it is?" the DJ shouted to the dance floor.

Hundreds of men and women howled and hooted then began stomping their feet. The music gonged then slowly turned into and irritating hum. Finally, it ended in a clash of symbols then exploded into a tribal beat.

Donovan could feel Charisse's heart pounding in her chest as she tightened her grip on his arm. Together they watched as the audience slowly dropped to all fours as their forms melted into something grotesque. Charisse jumped and looked up at Donovan.

His eyes had changed. They were bright yellow, like a beast, like the ones she saw in her dreams. Charisse slowly backed away from him. The fear welled up inside of her and tried to choke the breath from her lungs.

"It's okay," Donovan said as he extended his hand to her. "This is who we are."

"They're all," Charisse tried to say the word but couldn't.

"Werewolves?" he finished for her. "Yes. Them, me, you, your father. All of us are."

Then a sudden peace overcame Charisse. She felt as if she were floating in the clouds. The feeling wrapped it's warm, tender arms around her and guided her to the edge of the balcony. She stared at her brethren in wonder and amazement. For the first time since she could remember, Charisse felt like she truly belonged.

Hours later, Charisse and Donovan were curled up together on the couch in his apartment. He ran his fingers through her hair gently as they talked. Charisse had a hundred questions to ask him and a hundred more after that and she tried her best not to sound like she was interrogating him.

"So covens are like classes or castes, right?" she asked, thinking she understood his explanation.

"Yeah," he said. "Your father's so called family is made up of several covens. You and he belong to the highest one. The rest of us do as we are told when it comes to family business."

Charisse shifted her head on Donovan's chest slightly and listened to his heartbeat. She closed her eyes and remembered the last time she was here with her lover. She had been overwhelmed by the urges that seemed so distant now. She recalled how much she had needed him and the rawness of the heat between them.

As she relived that afternoon, she felt the familiar stirrings start to spark inside of her. Familiar but different. She wanted Donovan again, but there was a tenderness in her desire this time. She wanted to feel his body against hers as they moved as one, blissfully making love. That's what she wanted. She wanted to truly make love to Donovan and not just some hollow, unmoving fuck fest.

Donovan caressed her back through her t-shirt and closed his eyes as she explored all the contours of his muscular chest. Charisse pressed herself harder against him as she slid her hand up under his shirt. The firmness of his muscles beneath her touch kindled the fire inside of her. She curled her leg around his and pressed her pelvis against it.

Charisse cooed softly at the gentle shocks of pleasure that radiated through her body and filled her with a sense of erotic warmth. She felt a hunger slowly building inside of her. It was much different than the last time she was with Donovan and he could sense it too. This was the moment they had both really been looking forward to.

She lifted his shirt and placed a myriad of butterfly kisses on his toned chest. Donovan shifted slightly on the couch, slouching a bit so he could dip his fingers just under the waistband of her sweat pants and caress her silky, supple skin. She inhaled sharply and trembled lightly beneath his touch.

Charisse's tongue circled languidly around Donovan's aroused nipple. She ground her moistening mound against his leg more urgently. She knew he was getting the hint; no man could be that dense. It was frustrating her and she wondered what he really wanted.

Did he want the heartfelt passion that swelled inside of her like rolling waves or did he prefer that aggressive, mindless slut that simply fucked him with every ounce of pent up anger and frustration from two weeks ago? Donovan wasn't capitalizing on her growing desire. Charisse glanced up at him.

Donovan's head was tilted back on the couch and his eyes were closed tightly. He seemed to be enjoying the moment, as she should have been. She decided that maybe he just wanted to feel her passion and desire for as long as he could before they retired to his bedroom. Charisse returned her attention to his smooth chest and nipped at his tight skin. She'd be happy either way.

Donovan slid his hand further beneath her sweatpants and panties. Her luscious cheeks felt deliciously soft as he groped her round, tender, young ass. Charisse moaned softly and pressed back against his squeezing hand. His touch was delicate but powerful.

She kissed up his chest to the front of his neck. He squirmed at the touch of her supple lips on his skin as she suckled along his neck to the side. The heat was building inside of her, driving her to grind against his leg harder, rubbing her swollen nub against his solid leg. She could feel the wetness of her soaked panties against her smooth, bare flesh.

Charisse fought to contain herself. She was quickly losing control and told herself to take it slow or she would end up a feverish mess like last time. She let her hand loll gently toward Donovan's crotch. He took in a breath and held it in anticipation. He was just as hungry as she was, perhaps even more, but hid it much better.

"I love you," she whispered into his ear before sucking his lobe into her wet mouth.

Donovan was about to whisper his love too until Charisse's fingers closed around his hard, throbbing manhood and started to stroke him gently through his pants. He groaned lightly as she delicately took his earlobe between her teeth and tugged on it playfully. The shoe was on the other foot this time. This time it was Charisse that was intent on making Donovan want her more than anything in the world.

Her hips circled slowly against his leg, keeping perfect rhythm with the movement of her hand over his slacks. Charisse inhaled slowly, breathing in the scent of Donovan's desire. It fueled the flames that started to consume her inside. Then she stopped.

Charisse slid off the couch and smiled seductively at Donovan. His hungry eyes were glued on her. She ran her hands slowly down her cheeks and neck then the top that concealed her large, soft breasts. She squeezed them gently and whimpered. Charisse massaged her chest firmly before slowly lifting her top up over her head.

Her hard, sensitive nipples strained against her white lace bra. Donovan's mouth watered as he imagined drawing them between his lips. Charisse playfully tossed her shirt at him and drew her hands slowly down her body. Her hips swayed sensually to the tune in her head. She spun in slow circles as she worked her hands inside her sweatpants and began to slide them over her hips.

With her back to Donovan, she slid her pants further. The top of her white lace thong teased him. He imagined the soft fabric disappearing deeply between her scrumptious cheeks. He was dimly aware that he was rubbing his aching member through his slacks as he watched, completely enthralled, as Charisse drew her pants even further down then kicked them errantly away.

She shot in a sultry smile over her shoulder and saunter off toward his bedroom. Donovan sat still, frozen in place as he watched her tender ass sway gently with each step. He couldn't wait to join her. When she disappeared through the doorway, he rose from the couch. His throbbing shaft bulged beneath the fabric of his slacks, begging to penetrate her silky smooth flower.

Charisse's panties and bra flew through the doorway and landed on the floor in front of him. He picked them up and pressed them against his face. Donovan inhaled her musky scent from her slimy panties then quickly stripped out of his clothes and disappeared into the bedroom.

When Donovan entered the room, Charisse was waiting patiently for him. She was on her hands and knees on the bed near the edge with her head down submissively. She wanted him to take her, however he wanted. Soft and slow, hard and ruthless, it didn't matter to her. The moment he entered her she knew she would lose control.

She moaned softly at the grip of his hands on her hips. Donovan guided his swollen glands to her silky, glistening folds and entered her. Charisse dug her fingers into the bed in ecstasy as their night of passion-filled lovemaking began.

The next afternoon found Charisse in the back of her father's stretched limousine. Frankie sat across from his daughter with his window cracked slightly and nursed his cigar. They didn't seem to be going anywhere in particular so she figured they were going to have a talk.

"I heard you were at the Wolves' Den last night," Frankie said pointedly.

"You got your goons following me again?" Her tone was laced with a touch of venom. She hadn't come home until just before sunrise and hid her puffy, sleepless eyes behind her large, dark sunglasses. Frankie just shook his head.

"Obviously someone took you there and I'm sure you were told exactly what the place was," he started. Frankie tried not to sound condescending.

"Gossip, dear," her father continued. "It's not every day that my daughter goes there."

Charisse wanted to clam up. After a night of shock and sensuous lovemaking, she was having her doubts whether or not she was fully accepting the truth. Her father held something back from her, he always did, but for the life's sake, she couldn't figure out what it was. It gnawed at her like a starving dog would gnaw on a bare bone.

"So who's the guy?" she spat while struggling to stay awake.

"Charisse, I honestly don't care," Frankie said to her surprise. "I'm more concerned with your role in our family."

"I know, dad," she said.

Charisse knew what her responsibilities to her father were and wanted to get more involved but she had been rather distracted. The example she had made with Little Mike wasn't as bad as she thought. The moment she stepped foot into that room, a feeling of dread had come over her. When she was finished, she felt a twisted sense of satisfaction.

Now that she had a little closure with her newly revealed origin and her lustful cravings for sex had subsided, she felt that she could really dedicate herself to Frankie's will. Charisse slowly removed her sunglasses and looked at her father. He was waiting patiently for her to continue.

"I've been messed up for a while," she explained, "but I think I'm ready now."

"Good!" her father smiled and tapped the window between them and the driver.

They sat in silence as the driver steered them to an unknown destination. Charisse wondered what her father had up his sleeve. Everything he did and said had a purpose. It appeared he had already planned something for them. The anticipation was building inside of her and she felt that familiar pull from the unknown.

It whispered to her that she could handle whatever her father had planned. It held her in its gentle grasp, comforting her and giving her strength. It was intoxicating and Charisse admitted to herself that she missed it. She didn't fully realize the void that had been left in her after that afternoon with Donovan. Truly, the beast inside of her wanted its attention.

After a few turns, the car glided to a stop. The door opened and a rather slim, business-like man stepped into the limo with them. He was clean-cut and dressed like a banker. Charisse gave him a sideways glance before the door closed and they were on their way again.

Frankie introduced the stranger to his daughter as one Mr. Troy Langfork. The nature of his relationship with her father wasn't exactly revealed to her, just that he represented some people that her father did business with. They rode for what seemed like the entire afternoon while she listened to her father and Mr. Langfork haggle over details of a deal that was supposed to go down in a few days.

"So exactly what cut do you get?" Frankie asked.

"Not that it's your business but I'm well compensated," Troy replied.

Charisse was surprised at his sudden attitude toward her father. Through their entire business dealing, he had remained poised and very diplomatic toward Frankie's demands. Her father, on the other hand, seemed quite content with the sarcasm. Maybe the stranger had earned just enough respect to get a pass for that.

"So then 250 large, off the top, is pretty standard?"

Charisse's father's question bleached the man's face and made his jaw tremble. Her eyes darted back and forth between the two. It was an interesting twist.

"I spoke to your employer this morning," Frankie said.

He reached into his jacket and pulled out his heat. Troy's eyes widened and frantically looked around for a route of escape. There was none. Frankie crushed the barrel of his pistol into the slender man's mouth then a second time for good measure.

"He was confused why I said that 1.75 mil was a reasonable price," Frankie said while screwing the silencer into the end of the gun. "He thought the deal was for 1.5. Yet, the entire time we've talked, you've been spouting 1.75. Why is that?"

"My- my mistake," Troy stammered with a bloody mouth.

"We discussed previous deals too," her father said, shaking his head. "You should've taken your cheese and left while you could."

Before the man could say another word, Frankie lifted his gun quickly and pulled the trigger. Everything seemed to move in slow motion to Charisse's eyes. She watched as the bullet crossed the dozen or so inches between her father's gun and Troy's head. The stranger's face twisted quickly in fear just before the bullet penetrated his forehead.

Charisse jumped and shielded her face with her hand as the side of Troy's head exploded. Blood and brain tissue blasted her and she glared at her father with wild eyes. Frankie simply unscrewed the silencer and put it and his gun away as if nothing had happened at all. Business as usual.

"Dad! Fuck!" Charisse yelled at him. "A little warning would have been nice."

He looked at his daughter. Her angry stare left him to survey the damage to her clothes. On the outside, she seemed more upset that her relatively new outfit was ruined than to the fact her father just murdered some guy that was sitting right next to her. But inside, inside was a different story.

Charisse felt the animal in her stir again and the pang of lust that wracked her body. She closed her eyes for a moment to try and focus. She felt it seeping into her every pore, like before, like before Donovan and the years before him. Raw, unbridled lust began burning its way out.

"Charisse," Frankie said before she cut him off.

"Take me home," she growled and curled her legs up on the seat.

Before the door even closed behind her, Charisse bolted to the bathroom. She twisted on the shower then looked at herself in the mirror.

"What do you want?" she screamed at her reflection.

The ride home had been grueling. She fought the urge touch herself. Her entire body lusted for her. Her nipples anxiously begged her to touch them and her pussy cried out in pure, dark desire. Coming home only seemed to make it worse.

"What?" she screamed again before doubling over in a dry-heaving fit.

Charisse collapsed on the floor. The tile was cold and smooth against her naked body. She sobbed and eased her hand between her smooth, trembling thighs. Her body responded to her touch as she gently stroked her hard, sensitive nub, but her mind was blind to the pleasure.

Her tears pooled on the hard floor while she

cried. Her thoughts swam with questions. Why was this happening to her? What perverted force could possibly have such a strong grasp on her and why did it insist on ravaging her with lust? Charisse would have preferred pain or anguish over the bestial appetite that drove her uncontrollably to crave sex in any form.

As her crying faded to whimpering then finally ceased, she was overcome by intense pleasure that grappled her body. She realized she was lying on the floor and furiously pumping two fingers deeply past her dripping wet, silky folds. The lust raged through her, making her hungrier with each automatous thrust.

Charisse began to think about Donovan and the beautiful night they had together last night. As she focused on it more, the pangs dulled and her blinding lust faded into sweet passion. Her hunger subsided slightly as she relished in the recent memory.

The bed was soft beneath her hands and knees as she crawled onto it and waited for her lover. She could have slipped under the sheets or simply reclined back and waited for him with her golden, creamy thighs parted to welcome him in. No, she decided to give herself fully to him, to wait for him patiently and submissively, willing to let him take her as he wanted.

Then Donovan appeared at the doorway. His slender, muscled body took her breath away and she closed her eyes and dipped her head in submission. Her legs were slightly parted and her smooth back was arched, tilting her soft, silky ass up for him. Charisse could see the hunger in his eyes and felt the passion of his gaze as he drank in the angelic sight before him.

When his hands touched her hips and the tip of his throbbing manhood shallowly pierced her wet, waiting folds, she moaned wantonly. She could feel the love radiating from him and felt the heat of his flesh as he penetrated her slowly. His piercing drove her to a higher state, a plane full of passionate colors, pure euphoria.

Charisse gave herself to him fully. The tenderness in which he touched her sent chills through her heated body. They moved in unison, determined and passionate, slow then faster, but gentle and intense all woven together in a mesh of love. She had never experienced the glow of true lovemaking. Then again, this was only the second time she had been with a man.

Donovan's hips moved in tight circles and brushed firmly against her tender rear. This was everything he wanted their first encounter to be, but understood her unchecked hunger. He too had felt the pangs from the hidden, before he learned of his true nature. He too had unleashed his inner beast the first time he coupled with a woman. Perhaps that is why now, here in his bedroom with Charisse, he felt as vulnerable as her.

He shared her pain and desire, re-living his own ascendance to manhood as she bloomed into a woman. Donovan's eyes were wide open, locked on the woman writhing before him. He was dialed into her emotions and keen to her subtle keys. To him, they were the perfect pair, each undoubtedly knowing what the other wanted.

By now, Charisse had forgotten about her shower and had resigned herself to the comfort of her bed. She loved herself as purely as Donovan had and though she wished her recollection of their lovemaking would last forever, she was already feeling the pull of her approaching climax.

Charisse fast-forwarded the interlude. Donovan's sweaty body was on top of her. Her glistening, smooth legs were wrapped around his tapered waist, urging him to love her harder and faster. Their eyes never left each other's throughout the moment. She could feel his enraged shaft pulsing hard deep inside of her as it grew bigger, cocking itself to release the culmination of their heat.

Her teeth gnashed into her lower lip as she arched her back and relived Donovan's sweet release. Charisse clenched her thighs together tightly as the tremors of her orgasm thundered through her body. She could still feel the heat of Donovan's seed as it pumped violently into her, dousing the flames of her desire into warm, smoldering satisfaction.

Spent from her reverie, Charisse wobbled to the shower and turned it off. She collapsed on her bed and gazed dreamily at the ceiling. Somehow, Donovan was the key to controlling her intense hunger. She wondered if it were Donovan at all. Perhaps it was simply the love they shared. When she focused on their lovemaking, rather than their previous bout of raw, unbridled sex, she was able to control her urges. Charisse fell asleep with thoughts of Donovan swimming through her mind.

"Earth to Charisse," Frankie teased and snapped his fingers a few times.

Charisse blinked a few times and shifted her eyes to her father. His snorting laugh put a smile on her face. She was still caught up in the revelation she had last night and missed pretty much all of the one-sided conversation they were having.

"Sorry," she said. "Charisse here."

"Glad you made it back," Frankie quipped. "About yesterday, yeah, I'm sorry."

"I understand, dad," Charisse replied. She really did.

"But you know me. Matter-of-fact and I believe it's better to fix the situation immediately and completely rather than letting it spin out of control."

"Of course," she smiled deviously. "It also sends a very distinct message. Like preventive maintenance, eh?"

"Exactly," Frankie agreed.

He had been rather upbeat the last few weeks. He'd seen his daughter take more of an interested in their business and she didn't seem too faint of heart. There was no room for emotion or weakness when running an organization like this. Business was business. Frankie saw that everyone got their slice of the pie and took very good care of his people.

"Since you seem to understand where I'm coming from," he folded his hands on his desk and leaned back in his chair a bit. "I've got an important job for you."

Charisse's eyes seemed to sparkle in

anticipation. She'd waited for a long time to see if she was really ready to carry on in her father's place. She felt she was getting there and hopefully whatever this job was, she'd prove it to him, and to herself too.

12 RAPTUROUS NIGHTS

Prologue

Spring, the period in life where the earth seems to shine down and place its blessing upon everything; at least that is how Jessica saw it. The dogwoods were blooming and the lilies were just starting to open up. Life was abundant and rich, but for her, there was a vacant hole where real happiness should have been.

Her sister's newborn cries filled the dark interior of the cabin. She didn't want to get up, but she had too. Jessica was the closest thing to a mother the baby had. Her heart ached as she thought back on what had transpired. Her mother had suffered through the delivery, but had passed soon after. It had just been too much for her body to bear. She had known from the beginning that she might not make it. The doctor had warned her about her condition, but she hadn't listened. Now, not only was Jessica without her mother's love, but her newborn sister was as well.

Her father had abandoned them, giving the excuse that he just couldn't take on the responsibility of raising two girls on his own. That left the farm in her care, but her young hands weren't used to the managing of such a place out in the middle of the wild prairie. She was thankful for those farm hands that had remained on to work for her though.

Though it might have been true that her father had abandoned them, leaving them to only God knew what; it had been a blessing in disguise really. She'd grown a lot and learned how to struggle through the most difficult of occurrence, even though she was put to the task of the heaviest burden. Raising a child alone was not easy, especially when she'd not born the child herself, but rather, had an obligation to it.

She was young, only 23 and she, herself, had yet to feel a man's strong arms around her body, let alone his love. Now, she felt that was next to impossible to hope for. With the care of the ranch on her shoulders, and a baby to tend too, she saw no time for love affairs. The harshness of the plains winters, and then the rampant work in the spring left her very little time to seek out a husband. There were plenty of times she felt the farm hand's eyes riveted to her though. For her, she rarely paid them any heed, tending to what she need to.

There was never a time she remained oblivious to it though as she had to have an air of precaution. She knew what could become of a lone woman on the plains, even if she did have those who had promised to look out for her. They were still mean, regardless. In fact, Brandon, the boldest out of all of them had already admitted feelings for her. He had even broached the subject of marriage with her, but she was unyielding. She felt that there was just no way she could give herself to someone whom she was not in love with. He'd told her in time it would happen, but that wasn't what she was looking for.

She wanted to love before she married, not after. While he was awfully good looking, in that rugged cowboy way, he was far too demanding. She'd sworn that she wouldn't allow a man to control her, and she'd meant that. She'd seen her mother dominated by her father, and that was what had made up her mind for her. There was no way she was going to allow a man to pillage her home and her body. Not unless she wanted him too.

She fantasized about something more than simple love and marriage as well. She was enraptured by the fantasies she'd been reading about, and the many strange accounts she'd heard from neighboring towns left her wondering if her ideas were that far from the truth. There had been a number of young women simply vanishing from towns, no trails to follow, and no signs of injury left behind either. She knew that they weren't dead, but their whereabouts where a mystery to everyone.

In her subconscious, she longed for nothing more than to be taken away from the mess she was in. Of course, she had no intention of leaving her baby sister in behind, and as she sat, gazing down into her innocent eyes, her heart swelled with love for her. She wanted a better life for them both, one that could be fruitful and happy.

When her mother and father had been in her life things still hadn't been perfect but they'd managed through them. She remembered the verbal abuse the most, even though her papa had professed to be such a Christian individual. Her momma had always reminded her of what the hard plains life could do to a man. Jessica had just been too young to really understand.

She vividly recalled one time she'd had to go into town for her mom when she'd been real sick. She had wanted to try the magic elixir that the street vendor had been selling for a few days. Jessica had been wise enough to warn her mom that it was just some stupid, gypsy magic trick but she hadn't wanted to hear anything like that. So, she'd gone. On the way, she had caught a couple of young kids going into the woods holding hands. She knew both of them and had been curious as to what they were up too. Being as young as she had, she still wasn't so young that she hadn't begun developing urges. When her paw had found out about her behavior, her mother had tried to shield her, but to no avail. He had yelled at her and pushed her to the ground. When Jessica had yelled back her paw had plopped her a good one across the jaw. It had swelled up like a giant grapefruit and she had sworn to hate him from that day forward. In fact, the only real memories she had of him were bitter and hate filled. She was kind of glad he was gone now.

She glanced out the pined framed window one last time, enjoying the view and the quiet that seemed to hang in the air. The moon was full, illuminating the wide-open plain. For just a second she thought she saw a deer grazing at the edge of the wooded clearing and she couldn't help but smile at the innocence of it but then that emotion quickly turned to a frown. She realized her innocence had been lost long ago, maybe not physically, but on an emotional level, it was long buried.

A knock on the door interrupted her thoughts, but the little one was asleep. She placed her back into her tiny wooden crib, bundling her so she couldn't roll around and possibly suffocate herself. She then went to the door, peeking out of the tiny peephole, which had been carved into the heavy oak. It was late, and she couldn't imagine who would be intruding on her in such wee hours.

"Who is there?" There was no voice coming back, only the slight shuffle of feet.

"I said who is out there, what do you want?" She heard it then, it sounded like a scratching coming from the base of the door, but peering out again, she could see no one. Something told her not to open it, but she didn't listen. She had to know what was out there. Curiosity had always been her worst enemy. Her entire body tightened in tension, and even in a wee bit of excitement. Her mind was screaming at her not to open the door, but she couldn't stop her body from moving forward. It seemed with every inch her heart skipped another beat. She hadn't realized she'd been holding her breath until she was right upon it the door.

Raising the latch, she opened the door just a crack, and that was all the intruder needed. The door came crashing in, causing her to gasp and step back as it slammed against the cabin wall. A black cloaked figure entered, and without him even touching the frame of the door, it closed of its own free will. It scared her. She had no idea what was happening, or who this person was, or if they were even human.

She could feel her own heart hammering in her chest as the figure approached her. She couldn't make out his face at all, but there was something mesmerizing about the way he moved. She couldn't' take her eyes away, and she feared fainting. She felt the hand at the back of her neck before she even saw it coming. It gripped her firmly, but not in a way that seemed to be intent on causing injury. Through the cloak, she could make out glowing ember eyes and a man's face.

He breathed in heavily, and pulling her in closer to him, he inhaled of her scent deeply relishing in it even. To her it was just a little creepy that he seemed to be occupied with her the way he was; her scent, the smell of her hair, the scent of fear emitting from her pores. When his mouth closed on the side of her neck, she didn't move. Fear kept her bound to that position; well fear, and the fact that his hand was holding her there. She felt his tongue lick at her skin and it excited her in ways she'd never felt before.

In that moment she remembered her sister, and it was then she began to struggle against him with new found energy. She twisted from his grasp and darted down the small hall, knowing he was directly in behind her. She didn't dare turn back to look. Her thoughts were focused on her sister, and keeping her safe. She stopped at the bassinet, studying the tiny little life lying there so innocently. In that moment, she knew she had to do everything she could to protect that small baby. If she had to give her own, she would do it.

She felt him enter; and it seemed to get hotter in the room with his presence there. When she looked up, she was shocked to see him remove the cloak covering his face. She was met with the brightest green eyes she'd ever seen, but they seemed to shift back and forth between that glowing ember, and the vibrant green. She whispered to him, hoping he would listen to her pleas.

"You can't harm us, please. We are alone here. I am all that this baby has to count on for survival." He drew closer again, backing her into a corner. She searched frantically for something she could use as a weapon, and he must have noticed her desperation.

He grabbed both of her hands in his own, and pinned her to the wall, holding both of them above her head. This caused her breasts to shift upwards. As she was only in a thin sleeping gown, with nothing underneath, he had easy access to her desires. He was drawn to her, and one of his hands came out to caress her breasts, squeezing one tightly as his fingertips teased her nipple in a circular motion. He wasn't what he seemed, she was learning that very well. There was a lure about him, far surpassing any idea of him being some abomination. She felt herself being drawn into his web and she just didn't know if she had the power to disentangle herself...

Emblazoned Nights

He knew what he wanted and had been searching for it for quite some time. This girl and the wee babe; he had no plans of harming either of them but then she didn't know that at all. He could hear her pulse in his ears and it affected him in many ways, some not what he'd anticipated. Cedrick had been alive a very long time, unbeknownst to many who knew of him. He tried to stay in secrecy, as it was what his brother wanted, what he demanded rather.

Standing there, before the girl, he couldn't help thinking about his transgressions and how many families he had slaughtered through the decades; women, infants, peasants. That had been different though. It had been a time when he had not known how to control his thirst, his need to survive. He had a new hunger now. It was one that demanded he find someone to share eternity with, someone who he would eventually cultivate into his coven; or dare he think it again...his brother's covenant, as he was the leader.

Cedrick didn't agree with everything his brother was about though, and while he understood why he attempted to justify some of his actions, he could not account for why he had the need to collect concubines. Staring at the small framed woman before him, he decided then and there that she wouldn't fall to him. He also made it up in his own mind that the babe would be tended to, and when old enough she would be turned as well.

They lived by a code, whether he liked it or not. When they drew others in they had to kill them or turn them, it was just the way of it. He didn't want to enslave anyone but he needed something more. My brother has plenty indeed to keep him content; he shan't get this one too!

There was no question, his blood was running hot in his veins and his body was eager to break free from its restrictions. He wanted her. So many homes he had busted into in that fortnight, yet hers appeared to be the one he would leave standing, though not her. She looked afraid, but even so, he couldn't stop himself. He promised he would soothe away her fears, take it upon himself to make her obey him whether she consciously did or not. He could woo her, hypnotize her, whatever he wanted to do. He was no ordinary vampire, and that was why they all lived rather secretly from the others.

Their breed was considered an abomination really, half wolf/half vampire; much stronger and smarter than either of the latter mentioned. The transformation was controllable. They could all change at will and their gifts...at least that is what I think of them—well they were well manageable as well.

He took several steps toward her, almost laughing when she took an involuntary step back on account of his progressing ones. His eyes stayed on her face, taking in her full countenance and watching the many expressions change. He could hear her own thoughts and feel her inner turmoil. There was really no fear there, rather it was apprehension.

He was drawn to her, and one of his hands came out to caress her breasts, squeezing one tightly as his fingertips teased her nipple in a circular motion. He wasn't what he seemed, she was learning that very well. There was a lure about him, far surpassing any idea of him being some abomination. She felt herself being drawn into his web and she just didn't know if she had the power to disentangle herself...

Her eyes fluttered closed as her body built with a passion she became hypnotized by. She was caught up in a flame that she had never known until in that moment. Despite not knowing who he was, or if he was even human, she couldn't stop him, didn't want to. It was strange, a man coming into her home, her weak baby sister depending upon her to stand up before him, yet she was so willing to surrender.

Before she could make any protest, he had ripped the fabric open with one good pull, exposing her nakedness to his hot gaze. When his mouth moved to encase her hardened tip, sucking at it, and swirling his tongue across it, she couldn't stop herself from moaning loudly. Her body weakened and leaned against him as he seduced her there, in the quiet of the dark. Her voice escaped her in more of a wanting plea than a request for him to let her go.

"Please...mmmm. Please let us go." He continued to caress her, still not saying a word, but his eyes watched her every move, her every reaction to his touch. He nuzzled her neck, biting her gently there, as his other hand moved down her abdomen to cup her womanhood. He felt the heat of her rising up into his skin and it excited him. There, against her thigh, she felt him hardening, and he felt large to her. She moved against him, not because she wanted to, but because she couldn't stop herself. She was yearning for something she had never experienced before.

Cedrick was amazed at her compliancy to his touches. Any other woman would have fought against him, smacked him, yelled, but not her. There was something rather different, not human like. But then he knew she had to be, she couldn't be anything but a human. Still...taking in a deep whiff of her aroma, she smelled different even. She was amazingly sweet, and there was something almost daring him to bite into her, to even bleed her dry, or simply maul her. He controlled it though because there was more than this that he had planned. He was in a constant battle with his bestiality and his own small remaining sense of humanity.

It was another reason he sought someone to be with him, to share everything with him. He hoped they could change him, make him a better monster. He laughed inside at the irony of that concept. A better monster? How is something like that even possible? His hands remained against her skin even when he was lost in his own thoughts, reminiscing and considering...She must have known because she grew very still, watching him now and holding her breath as he gentled his movements.

It didn't last very long. He turned back to her in full focus, pushing his body hard against her own as he devoured her breast once more with his mouth. She felt his teeth biting into her flesh in different places, drawing blood and sucking greedily at her. Strangely, she wasn't afraid at all. In fact, she had dreamed of this many times, a haunting dream that had come over her night after night in the past year alone. She couldn't see why she should not allow it when she believed wholeheartedly that it might be meant to happen.

When he began to grind his hardened manhood into her, she felt the warm fluid spreading between her legs and that was something she was familiar with. She had touched herself enough to realize when she wanted something, and even though she'd never had a man, she strangely wanted him to take her. She even pushed back into him creating a deep rumbling growl to erupt from his mouth.

He gyrated his cock harder against her midsection, pushing and shoving his hips forward as if he were fucking her through her clothing. She could feel the wetness building even more, soaking her panties and petticoats. She was left with embarrassment because she knew good and well he could feel it to but it seemed to be pleasing him, making him attack her with more wild abandonment than before.

As he continued to press against her, moving his mouth to her other erect nipple, she bucked her pelvis forward, making direct contact with his hardness. She moved her pussy against him, almost riding his manliness. She thought she heard his moan again, this time less guttural and more human; but it still felt less than human. When her eyes opened, she noticed his had changed to the glowing ember again, but this time more vibrant than before.

He released his grip on her arms, and pushed her towards the bed lying in the middle of the room. When her shins made contact with the hard wood, she lost her balance, falling backwards atop the cushiony mattress. He settled himself above her, holding his weight slightly away from her smaller frame.

With one hand, he hiked her nightdress up and parted her legs. She could feel his fingers making a trail upward, toward her inner thighs. She kept her eye contact with him until the emotions provoked her to close them and her lips parted. His fingers circled her wet lips, sliding sometimes in between her velvet slit and teasing her swollen clit. As he applied more pressure, she opened her legs wider to him, arching her entire body in pleasure.

He pushed two of his fingers deeply inside

of her, finding the sweetest essence of her there, and toying with her passion. She felt his other hand move to his belt, unbuckling it, and pulling down his zipper. The sounds were magnified in the room, along with both their panting breaths. Sometimes his mouth came down on hers, kissing her hard to smother her moans that were now coming louder as she felt the pressure building in her body. He moved his fingers in and out of her, faster than before, seeming to enjoy her body meeting him with every finger thrust.

She'd never seen a man's cock, and when she felt his in between her legs, and his own hand sliding the head of himself against the outside of her pussy, she became delirious with passion. The thoughts of protecting her sister were long gone as he had her right where he wanted her. He was so big, and when his head entered into her, she cried out in pain, making him stop and look at her. He moved only a little, easing a little further into her wetness. Her tightness surrounded him, strangling his cock and driving him mad with the want to thrust hard inside of her, but something kept him from doing so.

She moved against him, her body sucking at his hardness, attempting to urge him deeper, but he could feel her maiden head that lay untouched. It was this that caused him to pull away. He was not going to deflower a peasant who seemed so different from others, no, not yet. He had other plans, and as much as he wanted to continue to claim her, to imprint himself onto her to make her his own, he wasn't going to. It was hard to pull away, especially after having tasted her flesh and drank from her. He slowly did though, knowing deep within him that if his brother had been there by his side he would have swatted him away and claimed her for himself. Anger filled him with the thought of it.

He decided he would gain from her some form of pleasure there in the darkness of that shadowed room, the quiet suffocating him, choking him almost. That was how bad he needed to be appeased. He pushed her towards him as he stood, deciding she could please him with her mouth and tongue, at least attempt to do so since he was fairly certain she had no idea where to begin. His cock stood out, the moonlight coming in the window highlighting it in a glow. He was so hard, and so long, she couldn't imagine the pleasure he could bring to her body, or could she?

He pushed her forward again, urging her to taste him, and it was then she herself realized that he wasn't going to take her that night. He wasn't going to claim her sweet budding virginity, but he still wanted to be pleasured. She licked the wet tip of him, tasting her own juices, along with his semen. It only took her a moment to begin sucking him, and she found she enjoyed the feel of him in her mouth. Never before had she done such a thing and shame sucked at her mind as her mouth sucked at him. She didn't stop though, just as she hadn't when he'd first started touching her.

As she moved along his great length, he

toyed with her breasts, flicking her nipples with his fingers, and squeezing them together at other moments. She could feel him straining as she went down to the base of him, feeling him glide down her throat. When he began thrusting forward, she nearly gagged, but stopped herself. She got accustomed to the movement, and her head met his thrusts. His growl of pleasure right before he came into her mouth caused her to move faster on him, sucking harder, and swallowing every drop of his manliness down her small throat. As he began to grow soft, he pulled from her and gave her his back.

She knew he was looking at the baby, and probably wondering whose child it was, but he didn't ask that. When he did turn back to her, his eyes were the vivid green again, and his clothing concealed his maleness once more. She couldn't stop the wanting though, and her eyes constantly drifted back to his crotch, wanting so desperately to reach out and caress him. She knew very well it was wanton of her, but in that moment, in the heat of it she felt animal like herself. Only her most carnal instincts were controlling her.

She didn't know what had come over her, abandoning her morals and pleasing some strange man that she didn't even know she could trust. Still, if he meant her harm, surely she felt he would have already brought it down upon her. No, she knew there was something else, something he was not telling her.

"What is your name girl?" It was the first time he'd spoken, and he had a husky tone to his voice. It was seductive and darkly alluring. When she responded back to him, her voice trembled, not in fear, but with desire.

"My name is Jessica. I don't know what it is you think you want, but please. You can't have me without my sister too; you can't take me from the child." He laughed, and when he did, it seemed to bounce from every corner of the cabin.

"Can't? I can do anything I want, and I can have anything I want. There is nothing, absolutely nothing you can do about it." With those last words, his mouth closed around hers again, and he sucked incessantly at her, intertwining his own tongue around hers, causing her to grow even weaker in the knees. He was in control, and he was driving her insane with passion. When she felt she could no longer take it, when she was at the verge of telling him to claim her, he let her go, turning to the tiny baby instead once more.

She watched in shock as he picked her sister up in his arms and then turned to her. He made no move to hurt the child, and he held her like someone who cared about that life, even though it didn't belong to him. When she held out her arms to him, he placed the baby there for her. But he came at her again, whispering in her ear.

"You are going to come with me, whether you want to or not, and you'll not make a sound. Gather some belongings for you both. I want you to know that if you try to alert anyone outside, I will kill you both where you stand. Do you understand me?" She nodded and moved around him. She went back to her room and laid her sister on the bed, while she grabbed a couple of saddlebags and began filling them with clothing items and other needs. He didn't give her much time. As she reached for some other things, he stopped her.

"No more, this is enough. Let us go." He nodded for her to move in front of him, which she did, after carefully picking her sleeping sister back up. When they stepped outside there was a dark carriage waiting. He pushed her inside of it before climbing atop the seat outside. She heard him whistle the horses into motion.

She took a quick peek out the curtain, and was in shock when she saw a couple of the hands lying in the dirt, with pools of blood all around them. Through the light of the moon, she could see that their throats had been cut, but it wasn't a normal cut at all. It looked more like they'd been ripped. She gasped in fright, and put her hand over her mouth to keep from screaming out in fear.

Laying her head back against the seat, she closed her eyes to try and wipe away what she had seen. She knew though, there weren't enough years that could erase such an image in her mind. It was simply horrible, and now, she was with the very one who was responsible. She had no reason to believe he hadn't killed them, but then, he hadn't tried to hurt her or her sister at all. His intent with her seemed more sexual than harmful. And she desired him; even then, even after seeing the carnage, she found she still wanted him.

They seemed to ride on forever, the

darkness swallowing them up. She knew there would be no one who would come looking for her. No one would want to risk their lives for a lone woman and small baby. Brandon had told her himself that no other man would want her, not with such a burden. He had made her feel like he would have been doing her a favor if she would have married him. As she grew sleepy, she couldn't stop her mind from drifting off, but the dream that took her was one she wished she could forget.

They were at the barn, and the other hands had gone out into the field to salvage what wheat they could for the season. They all had to eat and it appeared that winter they would be having more cream of wheat and corn stone biscuits than any of them really preferred. He had blocked her from turning away from him, his face looking blissfully sweet at first, until he had pawed at her.

His breath smelled of chew, and his body stank of sweat and filth. He was handsome but she simply wasn't drawn to his type. He had ran his hands up the front of her dress, fondling her breasts, before coming up to her collar bone and pressing her back against the barn wall with one hand.

"Don't cry, you know you want me just as much as I want you. This will be good for both of us Jessica, you'll see. If I can get my seed in you, well...we will have to marry then. You will give me a lot of children." She wanted to cry but didn't. She knew exactly what she was going to do if he didn't stop.

His tongue licked the side of her neck, and his breath blew in her ear, but it didn't turn her on. His hard, rigid pole of a cock, pressing against her pussy didn't make her yearn for him either, not even when he began thrusting his pelvis forward to pound into her pussy through her clothing. He looked to be fucking the air, but she could feel him, every time he moved forward, the tip of him hitting her pussy lips under her skirts. She didn't open for him, didn't make a sound. Her nipples stayed soft as he continued to try and bring them to excitement.

Finally, he backed away in disgust. "What are you, a cold, frigid woman? You don't like cock Jessica, is that it? Are you one of those lesbian things that like sucking other tits, and fingering another woman's pussy, hmmm? I bet you are." When he reached under her petticoats and tried to poke at her hole, she kneed him right in the groin, causing his hard dick to soften immediately. He fell to his knees in front of her.

"Let me tell you something Brandon. If I wanted cock, it sure wouldn't be your filthy stinking thing. You need to learn better manners, and how to clean yourself before you approach a woman. There is nothing about you that even makes me wet in between my legs, you hear me? Do you?" She spat at him on the dirt, turning abruptly and walking to the house. She stopped only for a second.

"Oh, and one more thing you cock sucker. I want you off my land, GONE! If I see you again I'll same as shoot you before I ask you any questions. I'm telling Tom too, so you best leave now." He didn't even look up. He grabbed his hat from the dirt and turned in the opposite direction, hobbling away. The only thought in her mind was that he had gotten what he deserved for trying to take advantage of her. When the door closed behind her, the baby crying took everything else away.

It woke her up from her light slumber, her sister crying in her arms. She talked softly to her, trying to calm her down. Eventually it worked and she went back to sleep, cradled against her chest. Jessica looked out the window again to find them winding their way up a dark path to a huge castle looking structure in the distance. It wasn't any place like she'd ever seen before and her body gave a sudden quiver. She couldn't imagine what would be awaiting them in such a place, what the people were even like, or if they were even people.

Emblazoned Nights: Part II

There were many faces milling about but they all appeared much different. The fog hung heavy in the air, and as Jessica glanced down at her baby sister, her heart swelled. In that instant she knew that the tiny little baby was the one good thing out of all the mess that was happening around her. When the carried eased into the circular dirt drive, coming to a stop she almost felt her heart stop as well.

Fear hung heavy in the air, and the people who she had thought were just that, people, now looked very different. They all were cloaked and wore masks to hide their faces, much like the man whom she now viewed as

her abductor had been. She shivered as the
carriage door was opened and he appeared in
the small opening. The size of him was
overwhelming and he even concealed the
moonlight. He reached out his hand to her,
and surprisingly she took it. However, as
soon as she exited the carriage he immediately
took the baby from her, handing it to another
woman he approached.

"Wait!" She tried to maneuver around him
but he blocked her, holding his hand up to
calm her down.

"She will be fine Jessica, believe me. You,
on the other hand...well, I haven't decided
what it is will happen to you as yet." He
turned his back to her and began walking
away as the crowd of cloaked figures began to
close in. When he turned to glance back, he
noticed her eyes were pleading to him to save
her. Unknown to Jessica was the fact that
they meant her no harm at all, though they
did plan to take her where all the others
before her had been taken. Cedrick had some
remorse for this and it was the main reason
he planned on finding his brother and making
his claim for her right away.

When he entered the main foyer he heard
several of the elders voices in the distance,
and his brothers own retort came back to him
loud and clear. It seemed to reverberate from
the high ceiling walls. The lighting was dim,
of course. None of them could stand the
harshness of too many candles or torches
burning, so every so often there was one old
timey lantern item hanging, just to barely light
the way. It didn't bother him any longer, as

he had grown accustomed to living in the dark. He did recall those days long past where he had enjoyed playing along the hillsides with the warmth of the sun at his back but that had been so long ago.

Once up the spiral staircase that seemed to go on forever he found his brother entering into a meeting with several of the elder clans that remained along their territory. He motioned to him but his brother waved him off, letting him know he didn't have the opportunity available to speak with him at the moment. Cedrick knew time was of the essence, as the girl would be being prepared for the ceremony. It was a tradition of sorts.

Any time a new captive was brought in; she was cleansed and dressed in the ceremonial garb. Following that, Davian, his brother, would enter and determine whether or not the female was viable for his needs. This time would be different though as Cedrick had already determined that, unbeknownst to his brother of course.

He'd be lectured he was sure. He was already prepared to hear the warnings of what it would be like to take a fledgling under his wing. He'd thought about all of that himself. He knew too that it was rather dangerous to be doing such a thing in the times they were living in. They were being hunted and several of them had been killed in the past few months alone. Not an easy task to undertake at all.

He spoke to several other brothers of the brotherhood before entering into his own chambers. The fire was stoked in the hearth and it was plenty warm in his sleeping quarters. Stepping over to the fire, he held his hands out, wanting to remove the cold that remained in his palms. It was to no avail. It was one of the things that he wasn't so willing to grow accustomed to, though centuries had passed. He longed to feel the warmth of the blood running through him again, giving him that vitality that he so sorely missed. His thoughts wandered as he stood there, sipping on the glass of warm blood one of the servants had brought to him.

It was their sustenance but like the others, he still lived for the hunt. He had no favor with drinking the blood from a glass. For him, as well as for his brother, there was simply nothing more inviting than the taste of human flesh beneath his teeth. A scowl formed across his countenance as he thought back, wishing he could somehow fight off the memories but he could not.

She had been so beautiful, surreal even, but that was in the past. He could still see her silver hair in his mind, the beauty of her face when she had smiled. Sadness filled him as her visage took him over, sending him back in time to a place he would have rather forgotten about. The girl, Jessica...she reminded him so much of her. It was probably the very reason that he yearned for her even then.

They had used to love to go riding together, both having had their favorite horses. He smiled as his mind traveled back in time, filling him with joy for that instant. If anyone would have seen him they would have thought it peculiar, but he wouldn't have minded, so lost he was with his hidden thoughts of the past.

Her hair was so long, it trailed down her back in thick waves, the silver of it hitting the sunlight and sending a dynamic sheen of sparkling beauty over her. The river lay just below them as they came to rest their horses at the highest peak of the cliff. It was midafternoon and they'd been riding for a couple hours, seeking out the most private of sanctuaries to share some time with one another. He knew her father disapproved of him but he disapproved of his entire family. They'd had a family history that went back way before either of them had even been born. The accounts he'd heard were indeed monstrous!

His chamber door opening drove him from his reminiscing and for once, he was glad. As he turned, he was met by his brother, his approach a little awkward. He wrapped his arms around his younger brother and then immediately moved away. He never liked to stay in close proximity of him as he had grown more and more unruly, antagonizing him mercilessly into brotherly combat quite often.

"Davian, I need to speak with you and it is rather urgent." Davian scoffed at him, taking a seat upon his bed rather nonchalantly.

"Yes dear brother, I am fully aware of what you need to speak to me about and I am all ears." Cedrick was a little taken back as he hadn't mentioned a thing to him. The surprise soon left his face though as it became clear someone had leaked the information. As they talked together, Jessica was being led to a chamber two floors below them. She felt drugged, and indeed, she had been. They'd given her psilocybin mushrooms, rare and wild mushrooms that lead to delusions and fantasies of the mind.

She was barely aware of them laying her across the bed, but soon the reality she thought she was in became something else entirely. The room didn't look anything like she'd imagined, and everything seemed so advanced, like something right out of a fairy tale. There was even a true running bath in the bathing room, but she could have sworn there was only a small, ceramic rounded tub when she'd first been brought in.

It took her breath away. She simply couldn't deny the room was gorgeous, and it was laid out specifically for a woman. On the edge of the silken bed covers was a thin, frilly chamois, with a note attached. It was from the stranger, and the only words were, "wear this for me." She couldn't believe it. Did he plan to seduce her during the night, maybe even in her sleep? The thought excited her, but she didn't hold out much hope for that. After all, he'd banished her from him, sending her off to God knew where. She had no idea what her fate was either. The short note certainly didn't add up...no, not at all. It didn't sound like a man who had plans to steal into her room and make love to her in the darkness.

She went to the balcony doors and threw them open, stepping out and deeply breathing in the night air. The rain had stopped, but there was a chill in the air. She gave a shiver, not for the cold, but for the feeling of something to come. She couldn't shake it but she could sense a change taking over her. Something was about to happen very soon, and it was going to be an occurrence that she would not be able to awaken from. She didn't know if she welcomed it, or feared it. Thoughts of a warm bath beckoned to her, and as she stepped back in from the cold, she made sure to lock the doors securely. For some reason, she just didn't feel right not securing them.

The bathroom was gorgeous, and its décor was that of the ancient baths of Rome. The wide mouthed rim was hand crafted, with heavy chrome handles shaped like claws almost. Iris had already started the water for her and the entire room smelled of lavender and sandalwood. It was relaxing to her mind and body. As the last of her clothing slipped from her body, and she stepped into the warmly scented water, she closed her eyes, allowing the fragrance to take over her senses. It felt so good, so much so that she felt she could actually fall asleep just like that.

She ran the loofah along her arms and across her breasts, gently grazing against her taut nipples. It felt good. She'd never had a problem pleasuring herself before, and certainly not now. The warmth, mixed with the texture of the sponge gliding across her skin heightened her senses and increased her already existing desire for a lover.

There was only one image in her mind though; one person that she wished so desperately would simply walk right into her sleeping quarters at that very moment. Knowing somehow that he wouldn't, she satisfied herself beneath the soapy water. As she touched herself, she sighed, imagining him replacing her own hands. She simply couldn't get over wanting a man she knew not a thing about. And the point that he had kidnapped her. She felt like she was speaking to a complete stranger but it really was to her own conscious.

She felt her climax building, her body tensing in pleasant sensations. When she did orgasm it was one of the most powerful she'd had in a long time, and it somehow eased away her tension, calming her and somehow catapulting her back to her normal senses. She'd never thought that a man she'd just met could seduce her mind and body in so many ways, yet he did. He was so perfect, and so very gentleman like. It was as if he were not even trying to be the visage of a man she wanted at all; it simply came naturally to him.

Stepping from the bath and beginning to dry herself off, she sighed yet again. He was just eerie in so many ways, but yet so wonderfully romantic, in a dark sort of way; even clever at the same time. She couldn't ignore it, and really, she didn't want to. Sleep was definitely getting to her, and it was already the wee hours of the morning. The bed looked so welcoming, and as she tossed the thick coverings back, it molded itself to her own body. The pillows were firm yet soft enough to imagine sleeping upon clouds.

As her eyes drifted shut, she was almost

immediately asleep. Her dreams came to her like mirrored images, so perfected, and almost life like. Her body moved under the quilt, tossing this way and that as her dream began to take flight. She was in the middle of a beautiful garden, and the moon was so bright, everything it touched seemed to glow iridescently. The gown that she was wearing was a pearlescent pink, and when she stepped into the brighter glow, it twinkled with a million diamonds. She heard a gurgling pond on up in the distance, along with the soft croaking of frogs.

Other sounds drifted to hear ears, but they were indistinguishable. A great breeze blew at her, blowing her hair back from her face, and twisting her gown about her legs, outlining her petite form. She heard a voice in the distance, calling to her, more like beckoning to her to come closer.

She didn't hesitate because the voice...it sounded so familiar to her. She saw him step from behind the tree line up ahead of her, but he was so very different now. His hair was longer, and his eyes much brighter than before. He was dressed so strangely as well. Cloaked all in black, with the felt of his robe obviously in silver, it billowed out in behind him. His hair had one single strand of silver through it as well, and when he held out his hand to her, she almost ran to him.

As she stood a simple arm's length away from him, it seemed awkwardly strange. His smile was almost too perfect, but she was still captured by his gaze. When she came even closer, it was as if the night split open and the sun began to rise. Birds start chirping in song, and flowers began to open around her. It was the strangest experience she'd ever had, and it felt so real. She reached her hand out to him, and he took it within his own. His was so warm, while hers felt cold, like death. She felt almost as if her energy was being sucked from her the longer she stood, connected to him. Still, she drew closer.

When their lips met, it was like a molten fire exploding in the pit of her stomach. He felt so very warm, so real. His body moved sensually against her in just the right way. When the kiss stopped, she simply stared into his eyes until he begin leading her deeper into the garden surrounding them. The grasses were so thick and plush, spreading out far and wide around them. When he began pushing her to the soft ground beneath her feet, she allowed him to, willing to give him anything he wanted from her. She laid there and watched him as he stripped in front of her, seemingly proud of his maleness. She felt her body building in excitement, the yearning beginning to take her over.

His mouth moved, she could see it, but his words were inaudible to her. As he leaned over her, his hair drifting across her face, she held her breath. His hands popped each button free on the bodice of her gown, and when he pushed it aside, exposing her breasts to his gaze, she could have sworn she heard him almost moan in pleasure.

His lips were warm against her, and his tongue taunted her, teasing her nipples to hard points of exquisiteness. She felt him pulling her gown up, his hand creeping up her thigh, and slowly parting her legs. It was then that she realized she had on no panties. It came as a surprise because she never went without such a proper thing. However, as his fingertips grazed across her already swollen clit, and he eased inside of her, she forgot all about being proper and dignified as she arched her back up so that her treasures were pressed tightly against his palm.

He watched her face as he pleasured her, moving in a way that touched the deepest part of her. Her moans were pleas for him to give her more, to take her body anyway he wanted too. Her nipples remained taut, now pressed tightly against his chest as he moved into position above her.

She could feel his hardness at her wet entrance, and she found she had never wanted anything so badly in all her life. When she felt him enter her, she bucked her hips forward, taking the whole of him inside of her. She cried out in sheer delight. He was even bigger than she'd thought, and when he began thrusting into her, harder and much faster, she was lifted up to a higher plane as waves of silken delight intertwined around her.

All the while she was being fulfilled she still felt rather strange. It was almost as if by giving herself to him, she was losing herself at the same time. It was true, she felt lightheaded, dizzy in fact. One of the times she looked at him his face had seemed to transform, and there was a glow about him. She didn't know if he was smiling at her or frowning in hate.

She felt him thrust even harder in her, moving faster than she thought was even humanly possible. Still, she allowed him to continue to take her, and as her orgasms rocked her body, over and over again, she became weaker with each one. His mouth came down hard upon hers; sucking so hard at her tongue, she was breathless.

She felt his body strain above her and felt his life giving seed pour forth within her body, her own pulling him farther in, an instinct she had no control over. When he was finished, he held his palm over her chest and a bright blue light formed there. It warmed her the longer he held it. She felt her energy coming back to her, but not enough. When she looked at him again, there was more silver in his hair than before, and it was longer, as if they'd been in the garden for years rather than mere minutes.

She tried to stay focused, tried her best to stay awake, but he was fading. She reached for him, but he was all but a glimmering glow, vanished before her eyes. As she lay there, unable to get back to her feet, she wondered if she were dying. Her body felt aged, and though not as drained as before, it still felt off. She felt herself slipping, falling backwards, and spiraling from where she was to somewhere else.

When she opened her eyes, she found herself in bed, the covers twisted about her. She had a sheer covering of sweat upon her body, and she smelled of flowers. She immediately sat up and threw the covers back, her hand coming to her mouth in utter shock.

There, at the base of the bed, where her feet lay, there were clear and distinct dirt smudges, and her soles were blackened, as if she'd been walking in a garden.

Her body felt alive with energy as well, not the kind that makes one feel lively, but one where it feels it was shared with another. She noticed dampness in between her legs, and pulling her dressing gown up, she could see the telltale signs of lovemaking, the moisture still visible on her thighs. A gasp escaped her as she threw her legs over the side of the bed, preparing to immediately cleanse herself. She had no idea what was going on, or how to explain it, but there was something definitely not right.

She swung open the balcony doors and stepped outside, shivering beneath the cold air that hung heavy in the air. Looking out in the distance, she could tell there was a garden. She could smell the roses in the air, but then she knew that was impossible. There was no way anything such as a rose could bloom that late in the season. It was then she turned to her bedroom door, wondering if she was free to go, or if she was a prisoner in this castle? She almost stumbled across her bed shoes as she halfway ran to the door, her heart pounding in her chest. She took a deep breath before trying the knob, praying that what she felt she would find wouldn't take place.

It was locked, and looking through the peephole, she could see no one on the other side. She pounded on the door, screaming to be let out. Unbeknownst to her, the door was soundproof, no one could hear her. However, out on the balcony, with her doors thrown wide, her voice echoed eerily in the night. It was a frightening sound to her one's own voice come back to them. She sat on the edge of the bed, wrapping her arms around herself as her awareness of what was taking place began to settle in around her.

She sat there for quite some time, listening to the faint ticking of the clock. When she looked around for some way of knowing what time it really was, she couldn't find where the sound was coming from. Somewhat defeated and feeling lost and totally confused, she wandered into the bathroom and stared at herself in the large mirror. To her, it looked as if she'd aged five years. Of course, she was still young, but her skin didn't have the same elasticity as before, and she noticed more freckles on her arms and across the bridge of her nose. Her hair was longer, as if many years had gone by without her being aware of them.

Sitting upon the end chair, she stared in silence, wrapping her arms about herself. She could hear what sounded like a million voices in her head, and she felt as if she were going slowly insane. A baby crying in the distance brought her back around. It was her sister but she could hear a woman singing to, softly at first and then louder. The crying soon stopped and she was left alone in the quiet once again. Sleep wasn't something she would even consider, not with what she'd been experiencing. It soon dawned on her that she'd been drugged but by what she didn't know.

She stared longingly at the heavy wooden door, somehow believing if she stared at it long enough, it would magically open. She knew that was only wishful thinking on her part. No one was coming, and no one was going to let her out. She could only sit and wonder why she was being held prisoner. She was too afraid to sleep, to worried that he would enter her mind again and take her over once more. She knew she didn't have the will to fight him at all, and she didn't even want too. She was infatuated with something that she couldn't understand, though she was starting to figure it out.

She kept asking herself what she'd done so differently from other women that had made this stranger so drawn to her. They had a connection, she could feel that. The dream, or what had felt like a dream, she couldn't deny the intimacy in that either. It was all happening so fast... Then it began to dawn on her. She recanted, in her mind, the creepy feelings of being watched, the sounds of someone following her night after night when she'd gone to the watering hole to water the pigs, the eyes in the woods.

She shivered, not from the cold draft seeping in from the balcony doors, but from the fear that had gripped itself around her heart. It had all been orchestrated so cleverly. Every detail had apparently been mapped out. The only thing missing was her not knowing whether this stranger planned on killing her, or taking what he wanted from her and the leaving her in a heaping mess with nothing.

So, she was no longer in the dark on her abduction. It was obvious her kidnapping had been pre-planned. The bad part, out of all of it was the fact that no one had any idea where she was. She sighed heavily as she threw herself back onto the bed. She knew the chances of him talking to her anytime soon were about zero to none.

She certainly regretted her actions now, or did she? She could feel the emotions building between her and her captor. She didn't call him by his name any longer, at least not in her mind. He was her abductor, her enemy. But, even so, she still wanted to see him again. She didn't know for sure if it was to just get some answers, or to feel him against her. She wondered if he was responsible for the dream, or wait...it hadn't been a dream, right?

Jessica was finding herself so confused, she didn't even know what time it was, let alone what day. For all she knew she could have been drugged and months could have gone by. It was definitely colder now, and the nights appeared longer. She was learning that as she lay there, thinking that the morning sun would surely begin peeking its head out sooner or later.

The hours had crept by slowly, yet she was still lost in an abyss she felt she was sinking deeper into with every second. Her mind seemed to be working against her, as she couldn't even form her own logical thoughts half the time. Probably just sleep exhaustion. She'd had very little rest, and if what she'd thought had been a dream truly hadn't been, then she doubted if she'd gotten any real sleep at all. She placed her hands above her eyes, massaging her temples where the pain began to ache once again. It felt as if someone were trying to pry into her brain and snatch away all her memories. She couldn't even recall the color of Brian's eyes any longer, try as she might.

Her body was sluggish and slow, almost like that of someone who had been sedated. As she placed her hands upon her chest, feeling the rise and fall of her own breathing, she heard a slight scratching noise outside the door. She moved as quietly as possibly, taking a position in behind it so that if anyone did come in, she'd be prepared. The only weapon she had was a pencil that was it. She knew it wouldn't cause much damage to the perpetrator, but it would at least buy her some time to get away—at least that is what she was hoping for. Still, glancing down at her hands, they were visibly shaking. She clenched and unclenched them, trying to stave away the nervousness that was welling up within her.

The door began to creak, and slowly open, but she had yet to see a body part come through the crevice. It was a voice...his voice in fact.

AUTHOR'S NOTE

Readers: I want to expand a few of the stories to see where the characters can be explored further. If there are any of the stories that you would like to read more about again, I'd love to hear from you!

Visit my blog at www.shongacy.com

Join my newsletter for free exclusive previews
http://www.shongacy.com/in

Follow me on Twitter at
http://www.twitter.com/shongacy

Like my page on Facebook at
http://www.facebook.com/shongacy

Discover my books at major ebook retailers everywhere.